# ORPHAN WITCH

## SCHOOL OF NECESSARY MAGIC RAINE CAMPBELL™
### BOOK TWO

JUDITH BERENS   MARTHA CARR   MICHAEL ANDERLE

L M B P N

DISRUPTIVE IMAGINATION

ORPHAN WITCH TEAM

## Thanks to the JIT Readers

Misty Roa
Diane L. Smith
Nicole Emens
Daniel Weigert
Keith Verret
Angel LaVey
Larry Omans
Micky Cocker

*If we've missed anyone, please let us know!*

## Editor
The Skyhunter Editing Team

# DEDICATIONS

### *From Martha*

To everyone who still believes in magic
and all the possibilities that holds.
To all the readers who make this
entire ride so much fun.
And to my son, Louie and so many wonderful friends who
remind me all the time of what
really matters and how wonderful
life can be in any given moment.

### *From Michael*

To Family, Friends and
Those Who Love
To Read.
May We All Enjoy Grace
To Live The Life We Are
Called.

# CHAPTER ONE

Raine smiled as the tall wrought iron gates of the school came into view. She had enjoyed Christmas with Uncle Jerry, but she was ready to return to school and start the new semester. While she wouldn't admit it to anyone, she had missed the freedom to wander through the library.

Agent Connor had been quiet on the long journey, which gave her time to think things through. She had been swept up in the new situation of the school and magic for the first semester, but now she had cleared her head. Most of all, she wanted to know why the FBI felt the need to put so much effort into watching over her.

She took a breath, but Agent Connor spoke first.

"You want to talk about why I'm here with you."

"Yeah." Raine watched the gates open. "It's not normal protocol."

The agent had waited for this moment. He hadn't wanted to bring it up first as that seemed more awkward.

The agency had given him the go-ahead to be candid with Raine as they felt she deserved that much. She had proven herself to be an intelligent girl after all.

"The agency feels that you are a person of interest." He felt her gaze on him. "We feel that you would make a talented agent and prove to be a valuable asset. With that in mind, I am here to watch over you and guide you."

"You're here to protect me if my dad's killers show up?" Raine smiled. "Does guiding me mean you'll help me refine my skills as an agent?"

He laughed at her boldness.

"You're still only fourteen, so there are limits to what I can teach you at this point."

Raine nodded, satisfied with this answer. She was sure she wanted to be an agent when she was old enough. She'd known that since she was a little girl. Everyone she knew and looked up to were agents, and she wanted to make the world a better place. Her magic had only reinforced that as it would give her an edge in her effort to help people.

A small number of cars were parked around the circular driveway in front of the grand mansion that formed the school building. Dorvu the dragon sat on the lawn and watched everything. A pair of witch twins argued with their mother over their need for a third coat. Raine looked for her friends, but they weren't in sight. She knew they would return that day, but they would take the train and the jitney.

Agent Connor handed Raine her bag from the trunk of the car and gave her a small smile.

"You know where to find me if you have any more questions."

She shouldered her bag.

"I'm sure I'll have more questions." She took a step toward the school. "Thanks for everything."

With that, she skirted the bickering twins and walked up the steps into the entryway. The headmistress whispered to Professor Fowler, who shook her head and sighed. They didn't notice her as she headed up the wide stairs toward the girls' dorms. She had expected to feel a pang of sadness at being away from Uncle Jerry, but the school felt like home. The now familiar bustle of students around her and the views over the grounds from every window were comforting.

Cameron came down the hallway from the boys' dorms with a big grin on his face. William was close behind him with a small smile. Raine hadn't seen the half-Ifrit look so relaxed before. The haunted look had left his eyes.

"Did you have a good Christmas?" Cameron tucked his hands in his pockets. "We got here about an hour ago. I saw your agent's car pull up."

"Yeah. Christmas was great, thanks. We ate far too much food, watched all the usual cheesy movies including the Christmas classic, *Die Hard*." Raine shifted her bag. "How about you guys?"

"It was fantastic." Cameron put his arm around his friend's shoulders. "The pack loved William and treated him like their own son, so he'll stay with us for every holiday now."

"It was amazing. I've never had so much incredible food, and everyone was so friendly." The half-Ifrit grinned. "I finally understand what everyone talks about when they get so excited about Christmas."

"That's amazing news." Evie appeared from somewhere behind Raine. "I'm so pleased you had fun."

Evie pulled William and Cameron into a light hug.

"Christmas was hectic for me. There was so much baking. I love baking, but I think I might be all baked out for a few days." She turned and hugged Raine. "How about you? Did you have a good Christmas?"

"It was perfect, thanks." Raine nudged her friend. "You'd best not tell the pixies you're baked out."

Sara came down the hallway toward them.

"Evie can't be baked out." She pulled a mock-horrified expression. "That's impossible."

Sara hugged everyone tight in turn.

"It's so good to have you guys back. I hope you had the most wonderful Christmas." She stepped back. "I had the usual stuff about why my magic hasn't come through yet, but I was given a beautiful dress and some amazing paints. I haven't decided what my first project will be yet. I'm thinking a dramatic landscape with a big storm overhead."

"Did you all have a good Christmas? We had snow in London, can you believe it? It wasn't the full white Christmas, of course. I don't think we've had that since the sixties, but there was some snow—enough to cover the trees and make the newspapers declare it was the end of time. The snow here is beautiful and Dorvu, the dragon— you've met him, haven't you? He loves the snow, and he'll frost the ground over so you can sled if you ask nicely. If he really likes you, he'll make an ice rink for you to skate on. Do any of you skate?" Christie beamed at them all. "Anyway, I have to run. We'll catch up soon."

With that, she walked away and joined a group of other

sophomore girls who were talking enthusiastically among themselves.

"I should drop my bags off. I'll see you at dinner?" Raine looked at the guys. "It's in an hour, I think."

"Sounds great." Cameron turned toward the boys' dorms. "See you at dinner."

Evie hooked her arm around Sara's, and the girls headed toward their room.

"Are you okay?" Evie looked at Sara. "Your Christmas didn't sound ideal."

The kitsune shrugged and patted her friend's arm. "It wasn't so bad, merely a little tiring. They mean well, and the paints really are incredible."

"My grandmother gave me the recipe for perfect brandy snaps. I hope the pixies will let me make them. They were wafer thin and snapped evenly, and the whipped cream filling was to die for too." Evie glanced out the window as they passed it. "I've never managed to get the snap part right, but I think grandma's recipe will fix that."

"What happened to all baked out?" Sara grinned at her. "You're already planning some baking."

Evie laughed. "I guess I really love it."

"Your baked goods are amazing. You could be a professional." Raine opened the door to their room. "Do you know what you plan on doing?"

"I'm not sure yet." Evie dropped her bag on her bed. "I'm torn between potions and baking. Potions could help more people, but baking brings light to the world too."

"I think I want to go into law." Sara began unpacking. "I'd like to be a defense lawyer, I think."

"I'll be an FBI agent." Raine set her now empty bag under her bed. "Like my dad and Uncle Jerry."

"Speaking of which." Sara sat on her bed and looked at Raine. "What's the deal with that agent? I know we've talked about it before, but we're close friends now so you can share more. It's odd that he drives you here and back home, so I wondered if there was another reason for him being here."

"He's here to watch over the school and to guide me into becoming an agent." Raine tucked her legs under her. "Or at least that's what he said."

"Oh, that's pretty cool." Evie sat down next to Raine. "So you'll be trained early?"

"I'm not sure about that." Raine chewed her bottom lip. "I mean, maybe? I think he might give me pointers and help me figure out what things I need to study. I know this is what I want, though, to honor my dad and Uncle Jerry."

Evie put her arm around Raine and pulled her a little closer.

"You don't have to talk about it if you don't want to."

She leaned against Evie. "I think I'm ready." She sighed softly. "My dad was killed by dark wizards. He was hunting them for the agency with Uncle Jerry. They ambushed him, and he couldn't get out. He died an honorable death and saved a lot of lives. They're still out there, though."

"The FBI will get them, right?" Sara moved to sit on Raine's other side. "I mean, they're awesome. They always get their man. Or people, I guess, in this case."

Raine smiled. "Yeah. I know they will."

CHAPTER TWO

Philip had arrived last and jogged into the dining hall in fear that he might miss dinner. He collapsed into his chair with a victorious grin.

"How is everyone?" He looked around the group. "Happy to be back?"

"Yeah." Raine took a sip of her water. "I actually missed this place."

"Same." Evie glanced at the kitchen. "I didn't expect to be happy about leaving home and my family, but I was."

"You know, the important question is, which movie will we watch on Friday?" Adrien grinned. "I believe we're due a zombie movie."

"Is there anything old and cheesy enough with zombies?" Evie scooped a spoonful of her potato and leek soup. "My family can cook, but the pixies really take it to another level."

"*Night of the Living Dead* was in the late sixties I think."

Cameron looked at his soup with some suspicion. "And that is an absolute classic."

"Does anyone have any thoughts or arguments?" Philip bit into his bread roll. "I think *Night of the Living Dead* sounds perfect."

"It sounds good to me." Sara finished her soup. "Don't forget the M&Ms to go with the sweet popcorn."

"Don't worry, it's on my list." He dipped his bread into his soup. "I'll bring extra Twizzlers too."

"Twizzlers for the win." Evie grinned. "They're the superior movie treat."

"Popcorn's the classic for a reason." Cameron pushed his soup bowl away with a smile. "Twizzlers are a good second, though."

"Hey, don't forget M&Ms." Sara folded her arms and looked at Cameron. "M&Ms are a classic too."

The friends continued with joking arguments throughout the main course, but everything stopped when the rich, gooey chocolate brownies and fresh vanilla ice-cream appeared. They each bit into the still warm brownie and savored the perfect balance of the chocolate to the sponge texture. It melted on their tongues, and the vanilla ice-cream had more depth than any of them had tasted before.

"I think I just had a piece of heaven." Sara leaned back in her chair. "Nothing can compare to that now."

"Wait until you try my brandy snaps." Evie took a long drink of her water. "I have a new recipe from my grandma."

"Damn, they're my weakness." Sara looked pained. "That will be a really hard contest."

"What are brandy snaps?" William looked from one to the other. "Are you allowed to bake with alcohol?"

"Oh no, they don't have brandy in. They have ginger and demerara sugar as the main flavors." Evie frowned at him. "Have you never had them at all?"

"You're in for such a treat." Philip squeezed his shoulder. "With Evie baking them, you know they'll be perfection."

William thought that over for a minute before he smiled.

"Could you teach me how to make them?" He looked from Evie to Cameron. "I'd like to make something nice for the pack next time I'm with Cameron's family."

She grinned. "I would love to."

---

The friends moved to the common room where they lounged on comfortable sofas.

"What's our first class?" Philip stretched his legs. "I haven't looked at the schedule yet."

"Dark magic with Professor Powell." Raine pulled out her schedule. "Followed by transfiguration with Hodges."

"Huh, that's actually really good." Philip smiled. "I expected to start with history, which isn't my thing."

"The Oriceran and military stuff is interesting." Cameron shifted his weight. "I'm not so keen on the more general things, though, and I'm useless with dates."

"I need to get my potions grade up this semester." Sara sighed. "I try, and I've done some reading over the

Christmas holiday, but I don't get on with potions somehow."

Evie squeezed her hand. "It's normal to have strengths and weaknesses. You're great at transfiguration, and I'm sure Professor Hodges has given up on me."

"He hasn't, I'm sure. You still get a B, right?" Raine looked at her. "I think he simply doesn't know how to rephrase things to help you. He knows you do your best."

Philip leaned a little closer to the others.

"When do we want to head to the kemana?" He looked at each of them. "We have tomorrow free."

"I think I've perfected my stealth spell." Raine grinned. "I might be good enough to put it over Cameron too."

"Oh, that's great news." Sara squeezed her arm. "I'm so proud of you. I know it hasn't been easy."

"Thanks. I feel like I've started to make real progress." Raine tucked her legs under her. "The gnomes in the library have been so helpful."

"Have you swung by there yet?" William glanced in the direction of the library. "I expected you to have an armful of books by now," he teased.

"I haven't. I plan to go there tomorrow." Raine stifled a yawn. "It's been a really long day. We drove here."

"Ah, yeah, you came with that agent, didn't you?" Philip looked at her a little more intently. "I know he's here to protect the school, but he's very involved in your life, what with driving you here and home. Are you some sort of FBI prodigy?"

"I don't know about prodigy." Raine looked away. "He is here to watch over the school and me, though. And he said he'll guide me on my path to eventually become an FBI agent."

"Your dad is the only FBI agent I've heard of who is a magical, and I suppose he's the reason you can be too. But do they take other people like us?" William gave Raine his full attention. "Magical people, I mean."

"They want to." Raine smiled. "I think you could be an awesome agent if you wanted to."

The half-Ifrit frowned and thought about it. He had considered that path over the Christmas period as he wanted to do something with real meaning with his life. His family didn't have his ambition, and he wanted to leave his mark on the world. Becoming an FBI agent would allow him to do something worthwhile.

"I don't know what I want to do with my life yet, but I feel that becoming an agent is a real possibility." William chewed his bottom lip. "If they'd have me, of course."

"I'm sure we can talk to agent Connor if you do decide to explore that option." Raine brushed her hair behind her ear. "He's a really nice guy. He'll answer your questions."

"Thanks, I'll keep it in mind." He skimmed his schedule. "When do your Louper practices start, Adrien?"

"The day after tomorrow." The elf rolled his shoulders. "Which I am glad of. My family put me through my paces over Christmas."

"With your combat magic and stuff?" Sara looked curiously at him. "Or did I miss something?"

"They were more focused on my physical fitness and capabilities." He settled himself more comfortably. "I am a little sore."

"Is that normal for your Christmas?" William frowned. "It sounds exhausting."

"No, they're not normally so enthusiastic." Adrien shrugged. "But I haven't been away from their guidance before."

"I think I prefer my baking family." Evie grinned. "I'm not really the combat model."

"I don't know, I think you could be pretty mean with a frying pan." Sara laughed at the image. "Professor Powell always tells us to make the most of our strengths."

The two girls chuckled at the shared joke.

"Did we agree on tomorrow for the kemana?" Cameron leaned forward a little. "I'm craving those nachos from Bubble and Fizz."

"They're so good." Sara's eyes lit up. "We definitely have to go tomorrow now."

"Is everyone in agreement?" Philip asked the group.

Everyone nodded or agreed.

"Shall we say right after breakfast, then?"

"It sounds good to me." Cameron smiled. "There'll be enough people bustling around to hide us."

Raine smiled and felt a warm glow of happiness as they arranged the details of their plans to sneak into the kemana. She had to admit that she had craved the sugar hit that came from Bubble and Fizz, and there was so much left of the magical place to explore.

# CHAPTER THREE

"Is everyone ready?" Philip held his wand and looked at them. "I think we should go." They had made it safely across the grounds and into woods outside the cave. They could now use the magical symbols to enter as there was a small lull in foot traffic.

Raine drew her wand and felt her magic within her. She focused on the stealth spell and pushed her magic into her wand. It came more easily now. It still took her a little longer than the others, but no one said anything. Evie gave her a small, proud smile as she formed the spell over Cameron. The shifter smiled and mouthed, "Thanks," before they turned and followed the others. Philip had made short work of the symbols, and they slid through and hurried down to the kemana with no problems.

By some miracle, no familiar faces lingered near the entrance that morning and it was relatively easy to slip into the crowds before their spells wore off. They headed to the east as opposed to the west, which they had previously explored. Raine walked a little slower than the others and whispered one of the few spells she knew by heart. She watched the magic overhead with its kaleidoscope of color. The crowds were dense around the main walkway that morning. Witches haggled with elves over some bright purple potions. Evie looked a little more closely out of curiosity and didn't recognize the name on the label. She made a mental note to look it up when they got back.

William formed a small flock of tiny butterflies of fire and light. They glittered and flickered over their heads and delighted everyone.

"You're doing amazingly with your magic." Evie grinned at him. "You've made such good progress."

"Thanks. Cameron's helped me center myself." He tried to shrug it off and hide his deep pride. "I'm glad to see my work's paying off."

"Shifters have some uses." Cameron grinned. "And I'm happy to help a friend out."

They took their time along the narrower walkways to the smaller shops where they paused to peruse the wares on offer. No one was really in the mood for shopping, but they enjoyed the freedom of the kemana. Sara hung back quietly and reached deep inside for her magic. The simple enchantment that she thought of as her own magic was present in a gossamer web of white and silver. Her kitsune magic, however, remained locked away. She could feel it but she had no idea how to access it. Sara knew she was missing something somewhere but still needed to figure out what it was.

"Raine, have you done much reading on kitsune

magic?" She looped her arm casually around Raine's. "I've tried everything I can think of and I'm at a loss."

"Not really, but I'm sure there'll be books on it in the library." Raine frowned at a Kilomea that insisted on walking down the center of the walkway. "Librarian Decker will be happy to help us look, I'm sure."

"Thanks, you're a star." Sara grinned. "I think I might have to get one of those huge ice cream sundaes from Bubble and Fizz."

"Oh, the ones with all the toppings?" Evie turned to look at her. "I thought about that, or maybe a banana split."

Cameron wrinkled his nose at the banana split idea.

"Nachos all the way." He slowed his pace a little to walk more comfortably with the girls. "I'm not much of a sugar fan."

Adrien felt as though someone was watching him. The hairs on the back of his neck stood on end and the familiar sensation of ice water trickling down his spine accompanied it. He glanced at the window to his right and used the reflection to look carefully at those around him.

He was right and caught a glimpse of the guilty party, but they ducked into a shop before he could get a good look at them. Adrien was sure he recognized them from somewhere, but he couldn't pinpoint where. Philip turned his attention to the elf.

"Have you been to any kemanas in France?" He stepped around a little witch girl who stared open-mouthed at a small dancing doll. "Are they like this?"

"Yes, they're similar. The atmosphere is more relaxed in the kemana under Paris, and the food is obviously different." He glanced around for the person following him. "But it is very similar."

"I guess a city is a city. They're all very similar at the core." Philip opened the door to the bookstore that acted as the front for Bubble and Fizz. "And there's something kind of cool about that."

The group gathered around the book that acted as a lever and Cameron pulled it. They descended the stairs and emerged into the brightly lit cafe. The fairies fluttered around with broad smiles on their faces as they carried trays of chocolate, ice cream, and pies. Sara took a deep breath and grinned at the rich, heady scent of sugar in various forms.

Their preferred booth was available even though the cafe was far busier than usual. A fairy waiter brought over a large glass bowl of nerds for them to pick at while they studied the menu.

"I think I need the dark chocolate and sour cherry sundae with extra chocolate and cherry syrup." Evie put her menu down. "I'm sure it'll give me a huge sugar high but it's definitely worth it."

"I have to go with cookie dough and strawberry cheese-cake," Sara said firmly. "How can anyone resist that combination?"

"I need savory." Cameron looked at the drinks section. "Although they do have Code Red Mountain Dew which I haven't had in forever."

"I prefer the original." Raine chewed her bottom lip and tried to decide what she wanted. "Although I think root beer is my drink of choice today."

They each ordered a huge ice cream sundae except for

Cameron who chose nachos. Raine looked around the room at the mix of people enjoying the niche cafe. A trio of older witches laughed about something while they shared a platter of chocolates. The Wood Elf in the far corner looked far too somber for such a colorful and sugary place. Raine wanted to know his story.

"He's really a spy waiting for his contact," Sara leaned over and whispered. "I bet he's an elf James Bond and he's saving the world right now. We simply don't know it."

Raine laughed.

"That'll be you one day." Cameron nodded in the elf's direction. "Clandestine meetings and saving the world."

She couldn't deny that it did sound good, but she knew working for the FBI wasn't like that. It was more poring over facts and evidence than sitting in fun cafes waiting for unusual contacts. Still, it was fun to joke about.

The shifter shook his head but couldn't keep the smile off his face when all the sundaes were delivered to the table. Each one was almost as tall as the person eating it. They all had a pair of sparklers which changed colors through all the hues of the rainbow. Raine picked up her long spoon and dug into her treat. The fresh lemon ice cream paired with the bold mint flavor tasted even better than she had dared hope. Her friends back in middle school would have been amazed to see her try something so adventurous.

Sara felt as though she were in heaven as she savored her sundae and was sure no one had made ice cream that good before. Everyone ate in a contented silence, each one surprised at the sheer quality of the food. They knew that the fairies there were good, but the sundaes blew them away.

When Raine had finished hers, Cameron nudged his remaining nachos toward her.

"Would you like one?"

She wasn't sure if she could eat one more bite, but the nachos did look good.

"Next time. I think I might burst if I eat anything else."

"I'll hold you to that."

"What are we doing next?" Philip leaned back. "Once we're able to move, that is."

"We shouldn't spend too long here. We'll be missed." Adrien frowned as he heard a voice that triggered memories from his childhood. "As much as I would like to explore more, the consequences of getting caught won't be worth it."

"Is everything okay?" Evie touched her fingertips to the back of his hand. "You seem distant."

The elf smiled. "I'm making sure we don't get in trouble, is all."

Evie wasn't convinced but she saw no reason to push the point. The elf would talk when he was ready.

# CHAPTER FOUR

To Head Librarian Decker's surprise, Raine entered with Sara. He hadn't expected to see the young kitsune walk willingly into the library.

"Good afternoon, Librarian Decker. I hope you had a nice Christmas break." Raine smiled at his poppy when it blew a raspberry. "We hoped you might be able to help us find some books on kitsune magic."

Raine had been surprised when Sara reminded her that she wanted to go to the library, but she was more than happy to go with her. They followed the gnome down the long aisles and stopped at a section full of amber and orange-colored books.

"You'll want the third shelf, mostly, although there are a few on the fifth shelf too." He put his hands behind his back. "You know where to find me if you get stuck. And I had a very nice Christmas, thank you."

Raine looked at the third shelf and pursed her lips while she decided which books seemed most sensible to start with. A few had their titles written in what she thought was Japanese. She had seen a Languages Club and perhaps there would be time for her to join that. Being fluent in multiple languages would be very useful to an agent after all.

Sara selected five books and Raine chose five more. They sat down at a quiet table near the aisle and looked through them. She wasn't entirely sure what she was looking for, but she was happy to read about a new and interesting topic.

Kitsune magic worked differently to witch magic as it came from emotions. Sara sighed softly as she read that kitsune were supposed to awaken to it naturally. The fact that she hadn't meant that when she was ready, she would need to go through some trials.

Having found the note on the trials, Sara switched gears and began looking for information on those. She wanted to be prepared for every possible outcome. Her magic had awakened but she still had little control over it. She was determined that she would find what she needed to do to access it fully, even if that meant reading.

---

Evie knocked on the kitchen door and waited. Tori opened it and pulled the girl into a deep hug with a huge grin on her face.

"Girls, Evie's back."

The other pixies surrounded her and hugged her tight. She couldn't help but feel that they had become her second family. They had been so kind and generous.

"My grandma gave me a recipe for her brandy snaps." She held the recipe out. "Would you mind if I gave it a shot?"

Tori took it from her and studied it.

"Oh, this is a good recipe." She handed it back. "Of course you can, dear. We'll give half of what you make to the teachers as their after-dinner treat."

Evie picked up her apron that Tori had kindly given her the previous semester and went to her workstation. A feeling of pride and happiness filled her as she ran her hands over the counter. That was her workstation. The pixies respected her enough to give her a space in their kitchen.

Tori brought the ingredients for her.

"I'll help you through it. They're more delicate than it initially looks." The pixie set the sugar down. "Have you made brandy snaps before?"

"Yes, but I can't get the snap quite right."

Tori put her hand on Evie's shoulder.

"Don't you worry. These will come out perfectly."

***

Raine lost herself entirely to the books. Time flew by and she jumped when the head librarian tapped her shoulder.

"Dinner time." He smiled in a fatherly manner. "You don't want to miss it."

"Thank you." She selected the books she thought were most useful. "Can I take these with me?"

"You go to dinner and I'll have them ready for you once

you're done." He took them from her. "Are you making progress?"

"I think so." Raine looked at Sara. "How do you feel?"

"Better, thanks. I think I have a better understanding."

"Well then, we can't ask for more than that." Joe appeared as if from nowhere and took the books from Sara. "You'd best hurry. The pixies are on top form at the moment."

"Thanks, Raine." Sara put her arm around her friend's. "I really appreciate you helping me like this."

"It's what friends are for." Raine stepped out into the corridor. "We help each other. I'm sure you'll figure it all out."

"I think you're right." The kitsune smiled. "I feel as though I'm finally on the right path. I kinda wish I'd gone into the library sooner. I was sure there was something wrong with me, though, but something's changing. I can feel it."

"Sometimes, the best things require the most work." Raine brushed her hair from her eyes. "We don't always appreciate the things that are handed to us, anyway."

"You know, I think you're absolutely right," Sara said.

CHAPTER FIVE

Raine had done some extra reading before breakfast to prepare for her first class of the semester. Professor Powell sat behind his desk, perusing something, when the students filtered into the class. He gave them a few minutes to settle themselves before he looked up and smiled. Raine noticed that he looked far better. He had clearly fully recovered from the poison that had plagued him before.

"As this is your first class this year, we'll begin with something easy. Shields." The professor looked around the classroom. "Shields are often overlooked, but they are very useful against a large variety of attacks. They can be thrown up and give you time to plan your own attack or run away. Don't forget, there is no shame in running away should you need to. It is better to live to fight another day."

Raine's protective instincts wouldn't allow her to run away if others were in danger. She understood the reasoning behind the statement, but she needed to keep people safe.

"We'll start with a small standard shield. Form the image of a clear barrier in your mind. Push your magic and focus it on that image. Speak the world *'clipeum'* loudly and clearly."

Xander looked at the students to see if any of them showed signs of confusion. Once he was satisfied everyone understood, he told them to split up into pairs and practice. "A small light orb will be enough to test the shield for now."

He didn't want to risk throwing fireballs or anything more severe around the classroom. They were still freshmen, after all, and their time for heavier magic would come.

Raine and Evie paired up.

"You try the shield first." Evie smiled. "Have you mastered the light orb spell?"

"Yes. The gnomes have been wonderfully helpful with that." Raine drew her wand. "Clipeum—at least that's a nice simple one to remember."

"I know, some of those spells are complicated. I worry I'll mix them up in a stressful situation." Evie formed her light orb and it hovered in front of her. "Are you ready?"

Raine reached for her magic deep within and formed the image of a shield in her mind. She pictured a simple clear shape that stretched from the ground to above her head. There was no need to get too complicated.

Her magic pooled into her wand and she guided it carefully. It stretched and pinged into the right shape. She nodded to Evie, who launched her light orb. Raine grinned when it bounced off. She felt as though she had a hold of her magic now. Her friends and the gnomes had been so helpful, and the library proved to be an invaluable resource.

Evie calmed herself and shifted her focus from the light orbs to a shield and was pleased to find it came easily. She was so proud of Raine and couldn't keep the smile off her face when her friend launched her light orbs at the barrier. Raine had worked so hard to achieve everything she had.

Sara pursed her lips as she wrangled her magic and tried to stretch it into a shield shape. It was usually a little difficult to work with, but she hadn't struggled like this before. No matter how hard she tried, it refused to form a cohesive shape and instead, split into threads and ribbons that looked as though they were taunting her. Philip put his hand on her upper arm. "Can I help?"

"I'm not sure." She tried to calm herself. "I don't know what the problem is."

"Well, what does it feel like?"

"Like my magic doesn't want to form into a shield. It has other ideas." Sara sighed. "That's ridiculous, isn't it?"

Philip shook his head. "Not at all. We know kitsune magic is different. Can you coax it?"

Sara took another calming breath and tried to ease her magic into the shield shape rather than forcing it. The enchantment turned soft and silky and stretched into a beautifully smooth barrier.

Philip threw a light orb at it and smiled when it bounced off.

"It looks like you need to work with your magic, rather

than trying to force it." He shrugged. "That sounds a bit philosophical, though, doesn't it?"

Sara laughed. "Just a little." She molded her magic into a light orb. "Ready?"

He had no problems forming his own shield. Magic like that had always come easily to him. Like Sara, he really struggled with potions. There was something about that style of magic that he simply couldn't master. He had read up on it over the Christmas break and spoke to his grandmothers. Grandma Annie had said he needed to calm himself for potions and that his ambition hindered him. Philip had thought on that for a few days and hoped he had figured it out. Potions class was after lunch.

Once Xander was satisfied that everyone had formed their shields he stood once more.

"Now, we will work on bubbles—or force fields, if you prefer. Rather than keeping something out, these keep something in." He gestured to William. "Would you form a small fire for me?"

The half-Ifrit swallowed and tried to ignore the gazes that turned to him. Fire came as naturally as breathing, but he didn't like reminding everyone of that. Still, he drew on his power and formed a small campfire in front of the professor.

Professor Powell formed a bubble over the fire with a quick flick of his wand. The blaze was contained in a neat shape. Nothing escaped from it, not even heat.

"It works with light orbs, even three or four." The professor looked sternly at the class. "I used fire to make your goal clearer."

He went through the instructions once more before he

let the students begin practicing.

Adrien smiled at William.

"Great work on the fire. It's not easy to form one from a distance like this." He shifted his weight in his chair. "Do you want to do the shield or the light orbs first?"

His partner didn't feel confident with either. His non-fire magic came as easily as his fire magic. He had practiced a lot, but his confidence was still lacking.

"The bubble, I think." He rolled his shoulders. "Yeah. The bubble."

Adrien exhaled slowly, and his magic flowed into four small light orbs. He bounced them around in front of William. The half-Ifrit frowned in deep concentration as he pushed his fire magic aside and searched for his other magic. It was a little buried, but he managed to find it. Slowly, he pushed it forward and maintained the bubble image in his mind. The elf had reduced the movement of the orbs to make it a little easier for him, and William appreciated that.

It took him longer than he wanted but the magic slipped over the last crack and the bubble was complete. Adrien nudged the light orbs with a little more magic to make them bounce more. They pinged off the field and demonstrated that William had done a great job.

"You're doing great." The elf grinned. "Ready to try orbs?"

Adrien mentally squashed the light orbs and William allowed the bubble to slip away. The vibrant globes came more easily now that the half-Ifrit could see his control had improved. They continued without any trouble and a growing sense that they really could do this.

# CHAPTER SIX

"We have potions after this, right?" Philip bit into his chicken sub. "Then we end the day with portals?"

"Yeah." Raine savored the fresh white bread of her sub. "Evie, have the pixies changed their recipes? I swear this food is even better."

"They've tweaked them a little." Evie sipped her water. "Honestly, I think they're happier. I've passed everyone's praise on to them. I'm not sure that they felt as appreciated before."

"Can we help with that?" Cameron asked. "I mean, can we send them a card or a wooden spoon or something?"

"I'm sure they'd appreciate it if you stopped by the kitchen and thanked them." she smiled. "They're really very easy to talk to."

"Does anyone have any ideas what type of potion we'll do today?" Adrien finished his Italian meatball sub. "I've only read up on healing and defense potions, so I'll bet it'll be something offensive."

Everyone laughed.

"I bet you're right." William shook his head. "We did defensive all last semester, so it really might be offensive stuff."

"I have Oriceran history." Cameron stretched. "It was very politically focused last semester. I hope we move into something more military."

"I tried to trade potions for that, but they said potions were mandatory for freshmen." Philip sighed. "I...er, I mean..."

The shifter shrugged. "I know what you meant." He smiled. "Don't worry, it takes a lot more than that to offend me."

"I hoped they would bring in a politics class. I feel that's something worthwhile." Philip pushed his empty plate away. "I know we have student council but getting a real grasp on world politics is something that has a wide set of uses."

"Have you spoken to the headmistress about it?" Raine finished her water. "Did she say no?"

"She said she'll think about it and needs to find a suitable teacher." Philip frowned. "I take that as a no."

"I'm sure she'll give it some real thought." Raine picked up her bag. "The headmistress seems very fair and reasonable."

"I don't deny that." Philip stood. "But I won't hold out too much hope."

## CHAPTER SEVEN

Raine had looked forward to potions class.

"Do you mind if I partner with Evie this time?" Sara looked at her. "She's offered to help me get a better grasp on the cooking terms."

"You can work with me." Adrien smiled. "I can help you with anything you get stuck on."

"It sounds good to me." Raine entered the classroom. "I think I've made good progress."

She sat beside the elf across from her usual seat and glanced at the recipe which had been placed on each table. Adrien's guess had been accurate. They would work on a small offensive potion.

He shook his head with a small laugh. "I knew it."

"It doesn't look so bad." Raine read through the recipe. "Is it one you've seen before?"

"It's a little like the flash bangs we made last semester. I think we'll master it okay."

Professor Fowler stood and fiddled with a bobby pin that failed to keep her mane of red hair out her face.

"As you've seen, today, you will make a sun flare potion. It's used to temporarily blind your opponent. You should be aware that it will blind you too if you don't take appropriate precautions. We'll try them in the courtyard behind the school."

A whisper went around the room. They were seldom able to try their potions and excitement rippled. The murmurs soon changed to how they would stop themselves from being blinded and what to do if it lasted for more than a moment.

"You'll be provided with appropriate eyewear." The professor looked for any indication of questions. "Begin when you're ready."

Adrien and Raine went through the recipe together. He made sure that she understood every step and they placed the ingredients in the order they'd be used.

"If you count the sunflowers into the water, I'll add the pinch of glitter." He picked up the glitter. "On three."

Raine took the sunflower petals and held them over the small cauldron which contained cold water.

"One. Two. Three." The elf dropped the glitter in as she dropped the petals in. "One more."

Adrien counted the petals with her. He wanted to be sure they had it perfect and hoped that working with her like that would help her confidence.

Raine turned the heat on the burner up and watched the water heat while Adrien peeled the yellow candle into thin strips of wax. He dropped each strip carefully into the cauldron in a counterclockwise direction while he hummed a song under his breath.

"What was that?" She looked at him. "The song."

He frowned. "Oh, sorry, I didn't realize I was doing it."

The elf's focus was absolute as he made sure the candle was pared down into the exact dimensions the recipe called for. She had to admire his perfectionist way of doing things. Evie had a more relaxed approach due to her experience.

Once the water boiled, they dipped matches into the honey and dropped these in at the east and west points of the cauldron. Ripples of gold flickered around the matches as the potion took form. The gold sank to the bottom, and Raine watched as a rich orange color stretched upward toward the surface, leaving pinpoints of color.

They watched in a comfortable silence as the potion bubbled and condensed to what was needed. They had reached the part she wasn't quite so confident about. Adrien handed her the glass stirrer and she called upon her magic. The potion needed only a small sliver, but she had struggled to push her magic into potions the previous semester.

The gnomes had helped her to feel her magic and get a stronger grasp on it. She had come far, thanks to their help. Raine gripped the stirrer gently and pressed her magic into the potion. As she did so, she felt the cool tickle of Adrien's magic stretch around hers. They watched as the potion thickened into a heavy amber solution.

"The recipe says we stir it for exactly sixty seconds, then pull it off the heat." He pointed at the recipe. "Do you want to stir or shall I?"

"You stir and I'll keep an eye on the timer." Raine handed him the stirrer. "You're far more precise than I am."

Sara chewed on her bottom lip as she watched everything Evie did closely. She'd struggled in potions the previous semester, but she was determined to get her grade up.

"This is a rolling boil." Evie pointed to the cauldron. "Do you see how there are lots of bubbles on the surface?"

Sara looked more closely.

"Yeah. And a simmer is much gentler?" The kitsune looked at the recipe. "With fewer bubbles?"

"Exactly."

She felt as though she now had a better grasp on the cooking terms. They were so natural for Evie, but Sara hadn't done much cooking.

"This is looking good, right?" She stirred the potion. "It looks like a thick amber liquid."

"I think so. We can't be sure until we test it in the courtyard." Evie checked that there was nothing left on the recipe still to do. "But it's as described."

"Are you telling me you haven't made explosive potions at home?" Sara nudged her friend. "Not once?"

Evie smiled. "Nothing quite this explosive. My focus has always been on healing."

"You'd make an amazing healer, you know."

She shrugged. "With potions, maybe, but not with full magic."

"Is that what you want to do?" Sara pulled the cauldron off the heat. "Be a potions worker?"

"I'm not sure yet." She put the flask in position. "I'm leaning more toward baking."

"The world needs more good bakers. People don't give professions like that enough credit." Sara poured the potion into the flask. "Baking brings light and happiness to the world. Sure, we need protectors like Raine will be, but we need light too."

Everyone had put their potions into their flasks. Some were closer to the ideal amber color than others, but Professor Fowler was pleased to see they were all at least on the amber spectrum. She led the students through the school and out into the courtyard behind the main building. The headmistress had placed a few extra spells around the area to ensure that nothing would be damaged should the potions not go entirely to plan.

Professor Fowler handed everyone a set of sunglasses with some extra shadow magic imbued into them to protect their eyes.

"We'll do this in alphabetical order." She gestured to Adrien. "You and your partner can start us off."

Raine held the potion as they walked to the front of the group. They turned to face the assembled students and she threw the flask carefully enough that it didn't land on anyone's feet.

To her delight, it exploded perfectly. The bright flash of light was pure white and blinding, and it lasted a good six or seven seconds. That meant plenty of time to get away or form the next attack if required. Adrien grinned at her and mouthed, "Well done."

It was a team effort, but she still appreciated the support and congratulations.

Philip and William were a little less confident with their potion. The half-Ifrit was sure that it should be a darker amber color, but he didn't know where they had gone wrong. They'd read the recipe twice to be absolutely sure.

When Philip threw their flask, it took a half beat before the bright explosion of light happened. It lasted longer than the previous students' had so William called that a win. Professor Fowler seemed happy with the results, so he allowed himself to smile. He was improving, and his non-fire magic had come more easily.

"We make a fairly good team." Philip grinned at him. "We might have to do this again."

The half-Ifrit had to admit they had worked well together. He wouldn't be opposed to doing it again.

There was only one potion that didn't go quite as planned. It emitted a high-pitched squeal when it exploded with light. When everyone's hearing returned, Professor Fowler explained that the noise had been caused by putting the matches in too soon.

Raine made a note of that in her notebook in case she wanted to add the squeal to future versions of the potion. It was certainly useful and would help disorientate any potential enemies.

## CHAPTER EIGHT

Agent Connor could see the way the students looked at him. Mara saw it too and sighed softly.

"Perhaps it would be a good idea to talk to them and explain your presence." She took a mouthful of her beef stroganoff. "We can do it in smaller groups rather than a large assembly. It'll be easier to answer questions then."

Bruce nodded and thought it through. He hadn't wanted to make a big deal out of his presence, but something needed to be done. Also, he worried about the impact on Raine. She was the FBI legacy, and he was there partially because of her. The students might not react too well to that.

"Okay. I'll talk to Raine first." He finished his meal. "I really am spoiled when I eat here. The pixies are amazing cooks and their food is the best I've ever tasted."

"We're very lucky to have them." Mara smiled. "I'm not sure what we'd do if they chose to leave."

"Live on sandwiches." Xander laughed. "I don't believe

we know anyone who could or would cook for us, and certainly not like this."

The professor felt far better than he had in years. Mara had relaxed around him again and he enjoyed her company. He noticed the small smiles that she gave him and he wanted to encourage their frequency. It was still early days, but he quietly hoped that perhaps there was a chance for them again.

———

Raine was returning to the library for the evening when Agent Connor approached her in the hallway.

"Do you have a moment?"

She frowned but couldn't think of a reason for him to come to her out of the blue.

"Of course. Is everything okay?"

"There's nothing to worry about but I've noticed that many of the students are curious about my presence. The headmistress suggested that I should talk to them. I wanted to make sure that's okay with you first."

"Yeah, sure. I think you can explain things better than I can anyway."

"Great. Is everything going well with classes and all?"

"I think so. I'm heading to the library to work through my homework."

"Well, I'll let you get on your way then."

Agent Connor left and Raine continued to the library. She greeted Head Librarian Decker with a broad smile.

"Back already?" He handed her another two books. "How was potions earlier?"

"Great. Your help has really made a difference. Thank you."

"It's a pleasure. You know where to find us if you have any questions."

Raine settled at her usual table and began reading up on portals and preparing her essay. Cameron soon joined her.

"Are you working on that essay for portals?"

"Yeah. Have you started yet?"

"I'm about to." He sat. "I'm a little stuck on the physics part of it. Do you think you'd be able to walk me through it again? I made notes, but I think I missed something."

"Of course."

Raine lifted a book from the top of her pile and scooted a little closer to him. She opened it to the relevant page and talked him through each step. He grinned when he finally understood.

"Thanks. You're really good at putting things in a way I understand." He retrieved his pen and notepad from his backpack. "I think I have a reasonable chance at this essay now."

"It's what friends do." She rearranged the books she needed so she could better read them. "Let me know if you need any of these books."

"Will do."

Librarian Decker watched as the young shifter settled down into his work. He had been concerned that he would be too wild and make trouble as he had in his previous school. Raine had been a good influence on him, though, and from what the teachers said, he had proved to be an excellent student. The head librarian was surprised to hear he hadn't tried out for the Louper team, but he knew that not every shifter would be interested.

---

Sara looked at her blank canvas and tried to decide what she wanted to paint. She had thought about it since she received her paints for Christmas. At first, she had considered a landscape with a large storm, but the image hadn't resolved itself in her head. Then, it struck her as the dragon swooped down in front of the window. She would paint a crumbling castle with a proud dragon sitting atop it.

"It's perfect."

Everything came together in her mind. She set up her mixing plate and arranged her brushes the way she liked them. The image was crystal clear when she picked her brush up and began setting down the base layers. It would take her a week to complete but she enjoyed the longer and more complicated projects. They were more satisfying.

She had the classroom to herself by the time she had the base layer down for the pale-blue sky at the top of the canvas. when she finally had the broad strokes of the castle down, it was almost lights-out. She had been completely consumed by her art and that left her feeling satisfied and riding a high.

A teacher came to send her back to her room and she washed her brushes carefully and left with a grin on her face. Everything was coming together, she knew it.

CHAPTER NINE

Bruce stood patiently at the front of the dining hall and waited for the students to finish filing in. After more discussion, it had been decided that speaking to everyone at once was the better way to address his presence at the school.

"Quiet down, please. Today, you are here to listen to Agent Connor, whom I'm sure you have all seen around the school." The headmistress glared at those who continued to chatter. "This is a short talk, so please focus."

The agent stepped forward.

"Good morning. I'd like to begin by saying that you are in no danger here. This is the safest possible place for you to be. My presence is not an ill omen and quite the opposite, in fact. As you're all aware, this school is run by the government, and they feel that you all have a great deal of potential. You have the ability to shape the world into something brighter and better. We hope that you will work with the government and the related agencies, such as the FBI, to do exactly that."

"I am here to work with Raine Campbell and guide her on her path to become the FBI's first witch agent. I hope that others among you will give serious consideration to applying for other government and agency jobs. We would very much like to have you join our ranks and help us make everything that much safer."

A senior elf raised his hand.

"Why Raine?"

"She comes from a family of FBI agents and she has shown great potential as an agent herself."

A sophomore witch raised her hand.

"Do we go to you for more information or..."

"I will do my best to answer any questions you might have. When I can't answer, I will give you the contact information of people who can."

A junior wizard raised his hand.

"Will you be mad if I join the CIA instead?"

Agent Connor laughed. "Not at all. We would all be happy to have talented individuals such as yourselves join our ranks, whichever agency you choose. Our aim is to catch the bad guys and keep everyone safe."

A freshman witch raised her hand.

"What if we don't want to work for the government and want to do something else?"

"There is no pressure to work for the government. We want you to be happy and successful. There is room for people in every profession."

Agent Connor looked around and didn't see any more

raised hands. The headmistress stepped forward once more.

"If you have any further questions, Agent Connor's office is two doors down from my own. You can approach him at any time during classroom hours."

With that, the students were dismissed.

"That went better than expected." Bruce turned to Mara. "I expected a more thorough grilling."

"I'm sure Raine has responded to the majority of the questions." She started to walk away but paused. "Do prepare yourself to answer the same questions many times over the next few days, though."

Mara had been right. Bruce had produced leaflets that answered the main questions on how a student might apply to the FBI, CIA, and NSA. He also had others on how they might try to enter the other government divisions. He was happy to find that the students had all been positive about his presence and excited by Raine's future.

The student council had been swamped with applications from students hoping to get some form of political experience. A lot of younger students had studied more of the country's politics and were eager to play a role in them. Philip had quietly asked about the politics classes with the headmistress.

Mara had tried to find a suitable teacher, but she hadn't succeeded. There were two leads she pursued in the hopes of beginning the classes the coming fall.

"I have not forgotten. I have a short list of teachers but

starting these classes halfway through the year is less than ideal." The headmistress smiled. "I appreciate your dedication to this, but I am doing my best."

Philip nodded, satisfied. He felt that this was something worth really sinking his teeth into. Even if no one went into a job directly involved in politics, to have a good understanding of them could have a large impact on their future decisions. He hadn't decided what he wanted to do yet. He had initially thought he would be an entrepreneur, but politics called to him. The idea of being able to influence policies and make the country stronger and better was one that appealed to him.

Some people had assumed that Philip was a pure businessman, but at heart, he wanted to take care of those he loved. The more he thought on it, the more he realized that he wanted to look after more than only those in his inner circle. He could do so much more and it was a matter of whether he did that through pure business or politics with a philanthropic side.

## CHAPTER TEN

Raine appreciated the spell the seniors had cast to keep the rain out of the Louper stadium. She sat on her seat between Evie and Cameron and felt warm and dry. It was the first game of the semester and the Cardinals were on track for the championship later in the year. William leaned forward to see what the team was doing. They seemed to be talking to the coach. He was eager to see the game begin and had loved watching the previous matches.

Adrien bounced on the balls of his feet while the coach reminded Matt for the third time that the Chicago Wolves were a very fast team and that they needed to really get moving for this match. Matt nodded in understanding and looked onto the pitch. They were all eager to start. Training had gone great and they were in high spirits.

The coaches were satisfied that the two teams were ready and let them go. The field slipped away and was replaced by a quaint European village. Adrien turned slowly and recognized Italian architecture. The sun shone from a clear blue sky overhead. The small village had been built near the top of a steep hill and each building had the traditional red-tiled roof and simple rectangular windows. Slender-trunked trees grew around the narrow paths between the buildings, each of which was barely wide enough for a car.

Matt listened to his shifter instincts and the coach's words echoed in his mind. The Bears would already be making their move through the village streets, but he wasn't sure which direction to take his team in. A soft breeze tickled his nose, and he picked up a scent—fresh oranges. Something told him that was important, so he pointed to the west and set off at a comfortable run. The team moved into their usual positions with Adrien at the back, the wizards in the middle with their wands drawn, and Etienne, Adrien's brother, up front with Matt.

Raine studied the scene and looked forward to visiting a village like that one day. She planned to travel when she could. The job for the agency would come first, of course, but there would still be time for breaks to explore the world. Cameron was more interested in what the rough, warm ground of the sparse woodland surrounding the village would feel like beneath his paws. He was used to running on softer ground through the alpine woods in the pack territory. He wanted to experience the difference and feel his muscles burn as he ran to the peak of the hill.

Adrien heard the echo of footsteps in the street above theirs. They sounded too heavy to be the rival team, but there was that possibility. Matt slowed the pace and looked for signs of what the footsteps might belong to.

Raine watched raptly as three clay golems matched the team's pace along a parallel street. The simple person-shaped clay forms were easily six feet tall. Her mind considered the best way to defend against them. They were, at their heart, earth magic and the clay would surely mean they were vulnerable to water. Explosives would be good, she thought. If she remembered correctly, Cody and Daniel's strength lay in fire, and she hoped they'd mastered enough other magic to tackle the creatures.

The team reached an intersection and Matt held up his hand to make them wait while he searched out what they were up against. He sighed when he saw the golems. His wolf instincts told him to tackle them but that was risky. If they managed to strike him with one of those large fists, he'd be out of the game. The monsters paused and looked at the team with their oddly blank faces. Matt could still feel their gaze when he looked away and it sent a shiver down his spine.

Adrien summoned his sword, but he wasn't sure how much good it would do against them. He spun the weapon in one hand while he called upon his magic and formed a small explosive spell. Daniel and Cody had the same idea. Etienne stepped slowly to one side and watched the enemy's reaction.

"Do we aim for their head or chest?" Cody looked at the creatures. "I feel the head is better."

"Agreed. You always take the head off zombies and things." Daniel wrapped his mind around his magic. "On three?"

"On three." Adrien held his explosive ready for use. "One. Two. Three."

They each released their spells as the golems lumbered toward them. Two struck the targets' heads but the third went wide and caught the edge of the building behind them. The first two vanished but the third ran at them with its arms outstretched. Etienne formed two more spells and launched them at the creature's head. It combusted in a puff of brown dust as Cody released his own explosive.

"Well done, everyone." Matt looked up the steep street directly in front of them. "This way."

The smell of fresh oranges called to him. He didn't normally associate the gold token with oranges, but his wolf instincts were sure they were tied together that day. They ran up the increasingly steep incline and the sound of voices reached them. The Bears were close, and it sounded as though they headed in the same direction. Matt led his team around a small church with an old bell tower perched on top and they emerged in a small fresh produce market. Oranges, tomatoes, olives and other fresh foods were stacked neatly beneath small dark-green umbrellas. There were no signs of the stall owners.

The Bears entered the small courtyard and made a quick bee-line for the olives. Matt didn't waste any time. He sprinted to the oranges, dug his hands between the fruit, and felt for the token. Adrien copied him, trusting that his team captain knew something. The elf's fingers brushed over something smooth and cool. He grabbed it and withdrew the token.

The serene scene faded away and the crowd roared as everyone cheered for the team.

"That was a record." The coach grinned at them. "A game hasn't been won that quickly before."

"They were amazing." Sara stood to make her way to the field. "We need to congratulate them."

"How did Matt know it was the oranges?" William squeezed past a senior wizard. "Was that a shifter thing?"

"I expect his instincts were involved." Cameron frowned at someone who almost knocked Raine over. "Our instincts do tend to be quite strong when they need to be."

It took them a few minutes to make their way down through the stands toward the team. Adrien beamed at them.

"Dude, those golems were creepy." Philip slapped the elf on the back. "You were fantastic, though. The way you threw that explosive spell."

"You were amazing too." Sara touched Cody's shoulder. "I don't think I could have performed that spell under pressure. You're such a great team and you make the entire school proud."

"You're a step closer to the championship, right?" William looked at the team. "You'll go into the quarter-final now?"

"That's right." The coach lifted his glass of scotch. "They're on a winning streak."

More students came onto the field and the team found themselves carried on the shoulders of strangers. They grinned with pride and excitement. Adrien couldn't believe he would go into the championship as a freshman. It was something he'd worked hard for but hadn't really expected to pull off.

CHAPTER ELEVEN

Raine returned to the peace of her room after ten minutes spent talking to a sophomore about the FBI and Agent Connor's presence at the school. She was more than happy to tell people about the benefits and overall good work that the FBI did, but she was ready for some peaceful reading.

Sara soon entered and flopped down on her bed.

"Tell me if is this something you don't want to talk about, but your dad died on the job, right?"

Raine put her book down and turned to face her friend.

"Yeah. He was working a case with Uncle Jerry." Raine tucked her legs under her. "They were trying to take down a dark magic criminal ring. The dark wizards made highly addictive drugs, acted as mercenaries and hired killers, and were thought to be trying to find a way to use dark magic to control others—like really horrifying zombies."

Sara's jaw dropped.

"Wow, that's awful." She scooted a little closer. "Are you

okay talking about this? We can talk about something else if you want."

Raine shrugged. "My dad was a hero. I miss him but I'm okay discussing it. I wasn't really supposed to know about the case, but dad and Uncle Jerry often gave me at least some details. I offered new insight which sometimes helped." She gave Sara a weak smile. "They still haven't caught that criminal ring. If they haven't by the time I graduate, I will catch them. I know I will."

Sara moved to sit beside her friend.

"I'm sure you will. You're intelligent and determined and you'll make an amazing agent." She squeezed her hand. "They'll be so lucky to have you."

"People seem really excited about the FBI right now. I think they'll receive many applications for agents." Raine chewed her bottom lip. "I'm sure some of the other agencies will get applications too. I feel like we can all make a difference. You know?"

"Absolutely." Sara stretched her legs. "I know I won't be an agent, but I think as a lawyer, I could do some real good in the world. I'm leaning toward defense to help innocent people out. Prosecution would be fun in a weird way or incredibly satisfying, but I think I could help more people by doing defense."

"I heard that Philip is thinking of politics with lots of philanthropy." Raine smiled. "He has such a sharp mind I think he could do a lot of good."

"William's thinking about going into the FBI with you." The kitsune nudged Raine gently. "The criminals wouldn't stand a chance if the agency had you both."

She smiled, pleased to hear that the half-Ifrit was now

definitely considering that path. He'd mentioned it before in passing, but it seemed his interest was genuine. It was obvious that he had a great deal of potential but she had thought he would choose a quieter job.

"Enough about careers and all that." Sara lay back on the bed. "Do we have a date and time for the next movie night?"

"Philip is getting the DVD tomorrow, so I think it'll be this Friday." Raine put her book on top of the pile of others as it was now obvious she wouldn't be able to read anymore. "I've only seen one zombie movie before, so I'm curious to see how this one compares."

"Zombie movies are all very similar. Except *I am Legend,* which I think might technically be a vampire movie."

"Yeah, I think that's a post-apocalyptic vampire movie."

"Well, never mind, then." Sara laughed.

# CHAPTER TWELVE

"I got us the colorized version." Philip put the DVD in the player. "I don't know about you guys, but I wasn't quite ready for a black-and-white movie."

William popped everyone's popcorn and Evie handed out small blankets she'd brought with her from home. Once everyone was comfortable in their preferred spot with a handmade blanket stretched over them, Philip pressed play.

Ominous music sounded over the opening scene of a car driving down a dirt road. Evie opened her pack of Twizzlers and passed one to Raine.

"Wow, they're really ramping up the tension with this music." William put some popcorn in his mouth. "They're making sure you know this is a horror movie."

"I don't like that guy." Evie frowned at the man in the movie. "He makes such a big fuss about driving to pay respects to his dead father. It's not such a big ask. I don't know, maybe family is more important to me."

"No, I completely agree," the half-Ifrit said. "My family was awful, but I still don't get his problem. I hope he gets eaten first. They're working very hard to make him unlikeable. All he's done is complain so far."

"Her hair is a really pretty shade of strawberry-blonde, though." Sara pointed to the woman on the screen. "If I ever dyed my hair, I think I'd go that color. It's very soft but still has a nice touch of red."

"I love your beautiful red hair." Evie squeezed her friend's hand. "I hope you don't dye it. It's such a gorgeous shade of flame-red—it's very striking and so very you."

"Aw, thanks, Evie." Sara offered her some popcorn with M&Ms. "Do you want some?"

"Which type of M&Ms?" Evie asked and peered at the popcorn. "Chocolate. Philip tried to get me the caramel ones, but he couldn't. Chocolate ones are awesome too, though."

"Ah, she had the good sense to kick her shoes off and keep running," Adrien pointed out. "In so many horror movies, they keep crawling backward. She's doing great so far."

"Is that guy a zombie?" Cameron frowned. "He looks like a pale man, and he doesn't have the zombie shuffle. Hey, wait, he's using a brick. I didn't think zombies had enough brain capacity to use tools."

"Well that's an argument worth having, isn't it?" Philip turned to him. "How much intelligence do zombies have? I mean, if you look at something like *iZombie*, she has her full mental capacity. Then you look at the movies like the, er, the one in the mall. The zombies are lumbering and don't seem to have anything past the need to eat."

"I don't like fast zombies," Raine said around a bite of her Twizzler. "I don't know, I guess I feel zombies are meant to be slow and groaning. The fast zombies are scarier, but they also feel less like zombies. At that point, they feel more like vampires or maybe even werewolves."

"I agree." Evie pulled her blanket a little tighter. "A lot of the charm of zombies is the slowness, I think. And the fact that they work in these huge hordes. You can build the tension slowly as the zombies gather around wherever the heroes are hiding out. They also have more of a chance to get away, so it makes the moment when one gets bitten have more impact."

"Don't forget the classic moment when someone sacrifices themselves for the rest of the group." Philip gestured with a piece of popcorn in his hand. "It wouldn't have the same gravitas if the zombies were fast. There's something about seeing the zombies move in closer and the inevitability of it. I don't know, I think it's a horror classic and has what people watch for. That real toe-curling horror of thinking what if that were you?"

"And that's why I don't like modern horror," Raine commented. "It's too close to home. It's far too easy to watch it and really put yourself in that position. I don't want to be truly scared. I want a laugh and a little thrill."

"This film definitely isn't what I expected," Cameron said with a frown. "I expected the really cheesy zombies with their arms stretched in front of them. Oh, like him." He pointed at the zombie. "See, he's got it right. I didn't expect them to have the knowledge to damage the car, though."

"I think we'll have to watch another zombie movie after

this to compare," Raine suggested. "This is still cool, though. I think it's more a product of its time and it reminds me of the swamp one."

"I like how well-dressed the zombies are," Sara declared as she picked out a couple of M&Ms. "I mean, look at him in his nice button-down shirt, cardigan, and slacks. You don't see the more modern zombies dressed like that."

Everyone laughed.

"Zombies really should take greater care with their appearance." Philip laughed again. "They simply don't care anymore with their holey jeans and blood-stained t-shirts."

"That house was very into floral designs," William muttered with a slightly horrified expression. "And look at those tiles—yellow with ivy designs growing up them. Interior decor was completely different back then."

"I prefer modern, clean lines myself," Sara agreed. "Nice simple colors and nothing too bold. Gray is too often overlooked."

"I agree," the half-Ifrit said feelingly. "People think of grey as a drab color, but it has potential to be really sleek. It's all about getting the right hues and balance."

"Exactly." Sara pointed at him. "Thank you. So many people love cream and beige, but that's not for me."

"Off-whites can really make a space bright and airy," Cameron interjected. "You can't go for a crisp, stark white, or at least not much of it. It looks too clinical, but a range of off-whites with some beautiful art can make for a striking interior."

"Cameron's room is stunning." William smiled. "He has small touches of metallic bronze and gold. It sounds ridiculous but it's a really peaceful space."

"How did we start on interior design again?" Evie laughed. "What happened to zombies?"

"The tiles did it." Sara couldn't maintain her straight face. "It was the tiles with the ivy in the kitchen."

"Do you think the woman's been bitten?" Evie asked. "She's acting really weirdly with that tablecloth."

"I think she's in shock." Cameron peered at the woman. "She could have been, though. I didn't see it, but I was a little side-tracked."

"If zombies surrounded us now, they wouldn't stand a chance," William declared. "We'd set them on fire."

"The smell, though." Sara wrinkled her nose. "Cooking rotting meat? No thanks."

"True," William responded thoughtfully. "We could explode them but that would be an awful mess to clean up."

"And things like that aren't covered in these movies." Adrien grinned. "They focus on the heroic bits."

"I'll continue to hope zombies don't surround us," Evie added. "It'd be too much mess and hassle. I have baking to do." A pair of hands reached through a gap in the boarding on one of the windows. "See, that's why you don't leave gaps." She pointed. "You're guaranteed to have a zombie reach through and grab you if you do."

"You can leave gaps to fire fireballs or guns or something at them though," Adrien commented sagely. "Like the archer holes in castles."

"Oh, is this the classic part where the group splits come from?" William asked. "I mean, all the other zombie movies I've seen have this moment. It had to come from somewhere."

"It's extra tension." Philip shrugged. "And it shows the value of different methods of handling the zombies."

"I get that, but the idea for it started somewhere," William pointed out. "Everything has a starting point."

"I think she must have been bitten." Sara pointed at the woman. "Look at her. She's really quiet and kind of glassy-eyed."

"I didn't catch it if she was, but it would make sense," the shifter agreed. "There'll be mayhem if she was."

"They're an interesting look into the human psyche and our approach to disaster," Raine theorized. "I mean, everyone has a different idea of what's best. Some people panic, some people go into bolt holes, and so on. Zombies are a great exploration of that."

"Or at least the broader types of people," Cameron agreed.

"What would happen if a shifter got bitten by a vampire or zombie?" Sara looked at him. "Would you still be able to shift?"

Creases formed between his eyes. "We had that discussion a couple of times over Christmas. One of those silly family talks people have after they've had a good meal." He pursed his lips. "We haven't really reached a conclusion. It would depend on the form of the zombies or vampires, I think. I mean, if they came from magic, that would interact with our natural magic. If, however, they were viruses, there's a chance that our stronger immune system would fight it off. On the other hand, our immune system could also lead to weird and wonderful evolutions and forms that no one thought of before."

"You guys really did think this through." Philip grinned. "I think that's awesome."

Cameron shrugged. "We end up having some weird conversations. It's a fun quirk about my family."

"We tend to talk more about business and related things." The wizard put his empty popcorn bag down. "Which I find fascinating, but I don't know, it'd be nice to have more fun, quirky talks sometimes."

"I'm lucky that I talk about everything with my Uncle Jerry." Raine finished her Coke. "We talk books, movies, music, weird theories—anything and everything."

Cameron grinned at William.

"Don't worry, you'll be dragged into plenty more weird conversations over the holidays with us."

"I can't wait." The half-Ifrit stretched his legs and looked at the tv. "I think I missed half that movie."

"I don't think you missed much." Evie shrugged. "It was a bit slow. Which zombie movie should we watch next?"

"What about *Day of the Dead?*" Cameron looked at the others. "It's very much on the border between cheesy old and modern, though."

"I'd be up for that." Philip picked up the trash. "But I won't argue if you guys want something older."

"No, I think eighties are good." Evie stood and folded her blanket. "I agree it's borderline, but I think it's still cheesy."

Everyone agreed and so it was decided. They were on a zombie kick for their movie watching. They each did their part to tidy the room and make sure it was clean when they left it.

"I'm so glad we started this." Evie looped her arm around Raine's. "I look forward to our movie nights."

There was a murmur of agreement throughout the group as they left the room and Adrien made sure the spells hiding the room were intact. Satisfied that they were all set, they headed upstairs into the main school.

## CHAPTER THIRTEEN

A few weeks had passed since the students had returned to school and they had settled into a comfortable routine. Raine stood with the head librarian in a quiet corner of the library with her wand raised.

"Now, remember to really enunciate. Don't fear the magic or the results. You won't hurt me." He reformed his shield around him. "I'm completely safe."

Raine had worked on a small offensive spell Professor Powell had taught her in the previous class. Her magic flowed well but it still didn't move sufficiently to have a real impact on her opponent. The gnome thought it was her concern over possibly hurting someone she cared about and he encouraged her to really push.

He had formed the barrier in such a way that she could see it shimmer and sparkle in the air. That reminded her that he was entirely safe. She pulled her magic once more and mentally spoke the words clearly and firmly. With her shoulders back, she steeled herself and pushed her magic through her wand as she spoke the words aloud.

The small explosive push of air hit the shield and made it ripple. It wasn't perfect, but it was a vast improvement.

"That was great, Raine." Librarian Decker released his shield. "How do you feel?"

"A little tired but I'd like to try one more time if you don't mind." She took a slow breath. "I'm getting closer."

He admired her determination and willingness to work as hard as was needed. She practiced her spells and magic with the gnomes two or three times a week and her extra work now paid off. Her teachers had mentioned her improvement in both skill and confidence.

"When you're ready." The head librarian reformed his shield. "One last time. I don't want to exhaust you."

Raine nodded and lifted her wand once more. She had seen how well the shield held and that gave her the impetus to really drive her magic into the spell. If she wanted to take down criminals as an agent, she couldn't afford to worry about hurting them.

She spoke the words clearly and crisply. Her magic surged through her wand and the air hit the barrier hard. He was almost forced to take a step back which made him grin with fatherly pride.

"That was fantastic." He dropped his shield. "Now, if you can do that in your next class, the professor will be very impressed."

Raine beamed.

"Thanks, Librarian Decker, for all your help." She looked at Joe who came to check how they were getting on. "And you, Joe. You've been very generous with your time."

"Oh, it's been a pleasure." Joe put his hands in his pockets and smiled. "Don't you worry about it."

"Don't be late for dinner now." The head librarian handed her the books she had checked out that day. "And we'll see you tomorrow."

Raine took the books and headed toward her room to drop them off before dinner. She bumped into Sara on the stairs.

"Do we have everything in place for William's birthday?" The kitsune looked around to make sure he wasn't nearby. "Philip's brought in the balloons and wrapping paper and Evie's baking the cake tomorrow."

"I have the books, and I think Cameron's got the music." Raine shifted the books in her arms as they were getting heavy. "We're sure he has no idea?"

"Absolutely sure. He thinks it's another movie afternoon." Sara grinned. "He'll love it."

"He deserves a really good birthday." Raine took a step toward their room. "I need to drop these books off before dinner. See you there?"

"Sure." Sara started down the stairs. "Catch you soon."

William looked at his friends and couldn't shake the feeling that something was off. He couldn't put his finger on it, but something had changed. It wasn't like them to keep secrets. They had shared everything over the past months. He shook the feeling off and enjoyed the wonderful chicken pot pie the pixies had made for them that evening.

Raine noticed the tension around the half-Ifrit's eyes

and the way he picked at his food. She wanted to reassure him that their oddness was a good thing, but she didn't want to ruin the surprise they'd planned for him. When Cameron heard William had never had a birthday party, the friends had made plans to change that.

They had little spare money for anything extravagant, but William had made mention of some books he wanted and a band he loved. The friends had pooled their money and resources to throw a small party in their movie room.

"How's the painting coming?" Philip looked at Sara. "That castle scene with the dragon you did with those special paints was incredible."

Sara blushed. "Thanks." She took the last bite of her pie. "I'm currently working on a ballroom scene. It's really intricate, which means it's taking a while. I'm enjoying it, though."

"I can't wait to see the final product." Philip pushed his empty plate away. "You're incredibly talented."

"Have you thought about selling them?" Evie drank some of her water. "They're professional quality. I'd understand if you were too attached to them, though. It can be hard to give up something you put so much time and effort into."

"I've been approached by a teacher to do a commission." Sara watched as the warm sweet potato pie formed on her plate in front of her. "I don't know if I can say who. I got the impression it was supposed to be a surprise."

Professor Powell had seen her paintings and approached her after one of his classes. He had asked her if she would be willing to paint a scene of the Blue Ridge mountains in spring for him. He said it was a surprise gift for someone but didn't specify who. Sara suspected it was the headmistress, given the way the professor and she looked at each other, but she didn't ask.

"That's amazing." Evie squeezed her hand. "I'm sure whatever you paint will be incredible."

"Thanks, Evie." Sara took a bite of her pie and closed her eyes in bliss. "Sweet potato pie is the best ever."

"No way. Pecan." Cameron finished his own slice. "Sweet potato is awesome, but nothing beats pecan."

"Apple pie with vanilla ice cream is a classic for a reason," Raine teased.

"It is, but it still doesn't beat pecan." Cameron shook his head. "It lacks the richness."

"You merely need to use the right type of apples," Evie pointed out. "You might be used to blander apples."

Cameron thought that over. He knew that she knew what she was talking about when it came to baking.

"Well, would you give me your recipe with the apples?" He gave her his most charming smile. "So, I can pass it onto my mom to try?"

"Of course. It's easy. I'm sure it's very similar to your mom's."

Whatever concerns William had had about his friends had dissipated. Everyone was relaxed and happily discussed pies.

# CHAPTER FOURTEEN

R aine walked to the movie room with William.
"Which movie did we decide to watch this time?"
He glanced at her. "It was another zombie one, right?"

"Oh, yeah." She fiddled with the cuff of her shirt. "I can't remember which one."

She had been given the task of bringing him to the party while the others set everything up. He looked at her with his eyes slightly narrowed, clearly suspicious now. Raine had been weirdly quiet and reserved all day, and the others had vanished immediately after breakfast.

Raine opened the door and the room was dark and silent. William frowned and looked around.

"I thought everyone was already here?"

He stepped into the room and Philip turned the lights on while the others jumped out.

"Surprise!"

The half-Ifrit laughed as happiness flooded his system. The room was filled with metallic balloons and a table was laden with his favorite cakes and candies. Then, the music began—his favorite rock band that he hadn't been able to listen to much of. It was perfect.

Evie came over with a pair of neatly wrapped gifts in metallic gold paper.

"We got you a little something." She handed them to him. "I hope they're okay."

William sat on the couch and unwrapped them, careful not to tear or damage the paper in any way. He revealed the books he'd spent a year looking for.

"This is amazing." He grinned and felt a little over-whelmed. "Thank you so much."

Evie hugged him tightly and was soon joined by Sara. Within seconds, he was in the middle of a big group hug.

"We wanted it to be special." Cameron smiled and shrugged. "Everyone deserves at least one special day a year."

"Do you want your cake now?" Sara gestured to the cake. "Evie made it."

"Well, then, I definitely want some." William stood. "Evie's cakes are to die for."

They gathered around the single-tier chocolate cake covered in chocolate ganache with fifteen colorful candles on it in a circle. Each one flickered purple and green, his favorite colors.

He noticed the small details that really made everything special. In that moment, he appreciated his friends more than he could say.

"Blow the candles out," Philip demanded. "Make a wish."

William took a deep breath and blew the candles out

while wishing he could keep his friends for many years to come.

He cut the cake into neat slices and bit into his own. It was even better than he had expected. The sponge was rich and moist and the ganache somehow fizzed lightly on his tongue. Then his favorite song came on and he sang along. Philip joined in, to his surprise. He hadn't thought of him as a rock fan.

The friends laughed and danced around the room, enjoying the party atmosphere. William couldn't keep the huge grin off his face. For the first time, he really felt as though he belonged.

---

They ran into the dining room, collapsed into their usual seats, and laughed.

"We almost missed it." Philip laughed. "It was worth it, though."

They'd lost track of time at their party and arrived in the dining hall two minutes before the cut-off for dinner. The pixies pursed their lips and shook their heads although they tried not to smile. They knew all about the party and had helped Evie make the cake extra special. Tori was pleased to see the half-Ifrit's relaxed demeanor and smile. He had always been more serious than Evie's other friends and that concerned her.

The pixies made turkey dinner with a small side of mac 'n cheese appear on their table and Philip sighed with relief. He really didn't want to irritate the pixies or make them feel as though they weren't appreciated.

"Thanks, everyone, for an amazing birthday." William ate his mac 'n cheese. "I can't say that enough."

Evie squeezed his shoulder. "That's what we're here for."

"And we had fantastic fun too," Adrien added.

The pixies gave them each an extra helping of crème brûlée as their added touch for William's birthday.

"Can you teach me how to make this?" Sara gestured to her crème brûlée with her spoon. "My mom would love this stuff."

"I'm not sure. I haven't really tried to make it." Evie savored her own dessert. "I can talk to Tori and the other pixies, though."

"That'd be amazing." The kitsune finished the last scraps of her dessert. "You're the best."

Once they'd finished their meal, they gathered up their dirty plates and carried them to the kitchen. Although the pixies usually saw to these, they wanted to let the kitchen staff know they were appreciated.

"Thank you for wonderful food and the amazing dessert stuff." William wasn't sure what to do with the dirty dishes. "I really appreciate your help with my birthday celebration."

"Oh, you're very welcome." Tori took the dishes from him. "We do love to help with things like that."

"Erm, would you maybe..." Sara chewed on her bottom lip. "Could you teach me how to make the creme stuff for my mom? I think she'd really love it, and I'd like to make it for her birthday over the summer."

Tori beamed at her. "Oh, we would love to." She looked at the other pixies. "What a lovely idea."

Sara grinned. "Thank you so much!"

"Thank you. We really appreciate how much effort you put into everything," Philip said. "Can we help in any way?"

"No, no, you go and enjoy your evening." Tori took his plates. "Enjoy your friend's birthday."

They left the dining hall and went to the social area. William ran his fingertip down the spines of his new books and smiled. As much as he enjoyed hanging out with his friends, he was ready to curl up on his bed and lose himself to one of the books for a couple of hours.

Evie nudged him with her elbow. "Go. Enjoy your books." She made a shooing motion. "We get it."

He hugged her lightly.

"Thank you again for everything."

William held the books close and walked up the broad stairs toward his room. It had been a long time since he'd relaxed and read a fiction book. He often read textbooks and non-fiction as part of his studies, but fiction was something rare and special.

He had the room to himself and took a moment to ensure his blankets and pillows were perfect before he cracked open the first book and began reading. It was the perfect ending to an incredible birthday.

# CHAPTER FIFTEEN

Raine used her wand to form the stealth spell around her. She turned and put one around Cameron. The spell came quickly and effortlessly. Her many hours of hard work had paid off.

The shifter grinned at her and mouthed a thank you. Philip entered the password and the group jogged hurriedly through the cave and down the stairs into the kemana. They had been dying to return to Bubble and Fizz. After a hard week of intense lessons, it was desperately needed.

The spells popped as Raine stepped into the enchanted city. The magic seemed particularly bright overhead that day. The thick ribbons of color glittered and sparkled with life. She took a deep breath and inhaled the heady scents of sugar, magic, and spices. Sara hooked her arm around hers.

"I'd love to see if they have an artist supply shop down here." She looked at the rest of the group. "I've read up on magically imbued paints and they sound like a lot of fun."

"That sounds good to me." Evie smiled. "I'd like to see if there are any baking supply shops down here too. It'd be nice to get a little something for Tori and the pixies."

"Shall we head to the north, then?" Philip looked down the main walkway in front of them. "I think that has more of the arts and craft type stuff."

"I agree." William took a step forward. "I think it's more jewelry and clothes around here."

They set off down the broad walkway and weaved between the groups of people. Witches in their early twenties laughed as they formed a large flock of butterflies and brightly colored songbirds. The winged creatures fluttered overhead and slowly changed colors. Raine slowed her pace and watched the way the hues began in the tip of the birds' tails and spread through their body. They started with a color on the blue spectrum and moved quickly through reds, yellows, greens and finally, back into blues.

"That's a complicated piece of magic." Cameron nodded at the birds overhead. "Some packs will pay for things like that for their parties. They're a colorful addition to any gathering."

Raine watched them for another moment and tried to figure out which spells were woven together to create them. She looked over her shoulder and saw them all explode into tiny fireworks sprays of colorful sparks.

The shifter kept pace with her and smiled at her interest in every little detail of their surroundings. When he had first arrived at the school, he had expected to be shunned and pushed out, but he had found a group of real friends. A second pack.

William tensed as they walked past the turn they would

have taken to go into the Ifrit neighborhood. He remembered the trouble he'd had there and wasn't ready to return. Evie threaded her fingers through his and guided him away gently. She would keep him safe.

Adrien glanced over his shoulder and saw someone watching him closely—a tall wizard with dark eyes. The tip of a tattoo emerged from the collar of his shirt. The wizard didn't flinch or look away when the elf held his gaze. He took a slow breath and ignored the disquieting sensation the wizard's attention caused. It made the hairs on the back of his neck stand on end.

He told himself that it was someone who wasn't entirely keen on elves. They weren't unusual. Everyone had their prejudices after all.

They saw the baking supply store first. Sara followed Evie inside as she was curious about all the things on offer. Toppings for cakes filled the near corner. They included everything from delicate stars, to small balls, and intricate flowers with tissue-paper-thin petals and rich, bold colors. Sara was in awe at the detail they had put into these decorations, all of which were entirely edible.

Evie, however, was far more focused on the utensils. She wanted something small for Tori and the other pixies as thanks for their efforts to help her with her baking. After perusing the usual icing bags, sieves, and other kitchen paraphernalia, she discovered spatulas with tiny paintings on them.

She lifted one with an autumn forest scene on the handle. Evie tilted it toward the light and caught the minute details that the artist had worked into it. It appeared that every leaf had been defined. Sara and Raine joined her.

"I think I'd like three." Evie studied them carefully. "I'm not sure which designs I like best, though."

Sara picked up a city scene with a sprawling metropolis. "Oh, wow, this is incredible." She looked closely at it. "They've put in every tiny detail. Some of those windows have curtains."

"Oh, hey, what about this one?" Raine showed Evie a scene with an array of complicated cakes and cookies. "Is that too blunt?"

Evie considered. "I think so. Maybe something more nature-y?"

They moved down the display a little and examined ocean scenes with wheeling gulls and small islands on the horizon. Evie finally settled on a serene beach scene, a forest scene with a carpet of tiny blue flowers beneath the vivid green canopy, and a rainforest with brightly colored parrots and tiny tree frogs hiding along the branches.

"These are beautiful. Would you like them gift-wrapped?" The older witch with silvery-blonde hair smiled. "It's no extra cost."

"Oh, please." Evie pulled out her wallet. Thank goodness they had learned to ensure they had a good supply of Ruby Falls coins. "Do you have any pale-purple gift wrap?"

"We do."

The witch wrapped the spatulas with practiced ease and added a thin silver ribbon around the center. Evie placed them carefully in her purse and they returned to the path outside.

Adrien leaned casually against the shop with his arms

folded and his lips pressed into a thin line. The dark-eyed man had followed them without making any attempt to hide the fact. The elf pointedly ignored him while waiting to see what he did. He didn't expect violence, but he had trained for many years and knew he could handle it if it happened.

The man finally approached him when he looked in a shop window at a pair of stiletto knives while the others were in the art supply store next door.

"Good morning. I'd like a word with you."

The elf looked at the man and said nothing.

"I think you'd be interested to know more about your family. They aren't as innocent as you have been led to believe. In fact, they are rather cruel and, on occasion, vicious."

Adrien sighed.

"Your family has a very long history and a singular reputation." The man stepped closer. "You're aware of that, aren't you?"

A Light Elf paused to watch their interaction. The dark-eyed man glared at him until the elf huffed and continued walking.

"As the youngest son, you must be treated as a child, thought of as immature and unable to fulfill your family's duties." The man waited for his reaction. "That must be difficult."

"Actually, I am very well respected in my family." Adrien smiled coldly. "Try again."

The wizard pursed his lips. "Perhaps you have heard of my family. The Corbeaux." He returned the elf's cold smile. "We aren't quite as notorious as your family."

"I know of the Ravens, yes. I have heard of your atrocious acts of cruelty. My family are guardians and protectors." He turned away. "Yours are thieves and murderers."

Adrien had been warned that other rival families would try to bring him around to their agenda. He hadn't expected it from the Ravens, though. They were on the verge of dark wizards. In public, they claimed to be protectors like his own family, but he had heard of the crimes they had committed.

He walked around the man and into the paint supply shop. He'd rather learn about paintbrushes than listen to someone try to tell him his family was awful. They had a long history of protecting innocents.

Sara was in her happy place, surrounded by paintbrushes of the finest quality. Canvases in every shape, size, and form were stacked along the back wall and paints lined the other wall. She chewed her bottom lip as she gazed longingly at the watercolors. She'd never been very good with them, but that had only made her more determined to learn.

Still, she needed to find something special for the painting for Professor Powell. She had heard about magically imbued paints that added depth to the color and gave the painting a more 3D effect. That would look stunning if used carefully with her usual paints.

She found them beside the oil paints. They weren't cheap, but they were within her budget. Sara ran her fingertip over the range of autumnal colors. The bronze would be a good option, she thought. The gold also added something, and she finally picked up a soft heather grey. They would complement the rest of her spring palette and add something without overwhelming the overall piece.

Her friends looked around with expressions of wonder on their faces. Raine picked up a small block of sculpting clay.

"You should give it a try. There's some quick drying stuff with little fibers that's easy to work with." Sara pointed to the clay near her friend's hip. "It can be really therapeutic."

Raine thought it over. She had never tried sculpting and she wasn't sure if she had enough spare time. She'd be breaking Smoke in first.

"Maybe next time." She smiled. "I'm definitely tempted."

Sara paid for her paints and the group made their way to Bubble and Fizz.

"Who'll split a pizza with me?" Cameron looked around. "William?"

"Pineapple and anchovy?" The half-Ifrit grinned. "Or maybe pineapple and pepperoni?"

"You're trying to horrify me now." Sara laughed. "Because they both sound awful."

"Meat feast with pineapple," the shifter countered.

"Deal." William grinned. "That sounds great."

Philip arranged to share his nachos with Adrien on the condition that they got extra cheese. The girls all agreed to split a Hershey's platter and a pepperoni pizza with triple cheese.

To their surprise, Bubble and Fizz was quiet when they walked in. They had expected it to bustle with business given that it was a Saturday morning.

The fairy waiter placed a bowl of small chocolates in

the middle of the table and gave them a brilliant smile when they ordered. Raine had looked forward to their strawberry milkshake all week. It was a simple pleasure.

"Has anyone done the homework on the New York kemana yet?" Philip selected a chocolate. "Does this go toward that?"

Sara laughed. "Wouldn't that be great?" She looked around the cafe. "No, I haven't started yet. I haven't figured out my angle."

"How about you, Raine?" Cameron smiled at her. "Do you have your essay written?"

"Not yet. I thought about tackling the history of the Kilomea there." She shrugged. "I've had a hard time finding books on it, though."

"I wanted to do a piece on the relationship between the Kilomea and the Willen." The shifter leaned a little closer to Raine. "Maybe we could work together?"

"That sounds great." She took a couple of the chocolates. "These are so good. Any idea what they are?"

"They're our own brand." The fairy placed the pizzas down. "I'm glad you enjoy them."

"I thought of taking more of a business perspective with that essay," Philip said. "The New York City kemana is an absolute hub of business and there have been some incredible developments from there."

"I don't think I have enough of a business brain for that." William bit into his slice of pizza. "I might take more of a historical view and do something on the growth of the kemana since it began."

"How long do we have?" Adrien wiped some sauce from his chin. "Two weeks?"

"Yeah. Which I thought was pretty generous." Raine leaned back and sipped her milkshake. "The essay is only three thousand words."

"Only." Evie laughed. "You make it sound like an hour's work."

"We'll have far longer essays in college," Raine responded. "And I'd rather have an essay over a lab report."

Philip groaned. "Do we owe Professor Fowler any lab reports?"

"No, you're good," Sara assured him. "Thankfully, she only does one a semester."

"I don't know what it is, but I can't get my head around them." Raine chewed on her straw for a moment. "I much prefer the flow of essays."

She looked around the brightly lit cafe and smiled. More people now filled the tables and the fairies seemed particularly happy. Their wings fluttered when they took the orders from the new arrivals. A pair of younger women danced along to the song that came on. Bubble and Fizz was pure happiness.

# CHAPTER SIXTEEN

R aine looked at the miserable rainy weather in dismay. Smoke hated being wet and always pranced and pulled back toward the barn. She didn't look forward to convincing him to go through water jumps. They had begun work on backing him. As she knew he'd only prance and be a nuisance outside, she had to do slower, quieter work in the stall.

He was good about having a rug on but now, she worked up to a tighter surcingle and the weight of a saddle. Once the weather cleared a little, she planned to work him on long reins with the surcingle so he would grow accustomed to the contact on the bit. She would also teach him to turn and stop before she got on.

Smoke whinnied for her when she walked into the barn. He stretched his head over the top of his door and called to her. She smiled and collected the cheap saddle and surcingle on her way to his stall. He had come so far since she'd first met him the previous fall.

Raine rubbed his face and told him to move back. It had taken a while and a good deal of encouragement to teach him not to try to barge out of his stable and he now stepped back. She entered the stall and rubbed his withers in greeting. He sniffed her hair and once they were both relaxed, she started with the saddle. She placed it carefully in the correct position and encouraged him to look at it and sniff it.

To her relief, the young horse was entirely unfazed by the weight. She removed it and placed the surcingle in place around his belly. He looked at her as she tightened it but he didn't react any more than that. Some older and more experienced horses would take a big breath and make their belly as big as possible to stop the girth from tightening.

She put Smoke's head collar on and led him through the stable and outside with the surcingle on. He looked pointedly at the barn after a few steps but Raine didn't want to encourage that too much. She didn't intend to work him too hard but she would do at least a couple of small exercises.

He heaved a great sigh as she opened the gate and he understood that he would be stuck in the rain.

---

Sara had spent hours finding photographs of the Blue Ridge mountains in the spring and wandered the school grounds to study the view. She was finally satisfied that she had the image set well enough in her mind to begin painting. A flutter of nerves formed in her stomach as she realized this was her first commission. She hoped it was the first of many.

Her mind cleared and left only the image she wanted to paint. The base layer was always her least favorite. It was large and blocky but necessary. The details were where Sara really started to enjoy her art. She loved the way that a tiny touch of color could have such a huge impact on the overall piece.

It took her a few hours to get the entire base down. The canvas Professor Powell had chosen was almost the largest she'd ever worked with. That gave her more freedom, though, and she appreciated that. When the base was done, she stepped back and smiled as she saw where the finer points would go the next day. It looked like nothing more than broad smudges of color to a non-painter, but Sara saw its full potential.

---

Evie held the three wrapped spatulas in her hand and stepped into the kitchen. Bright, happy music played over the hidden speakers and the pixies danced around the large table in the center of the room. Their faces were pictures of happiness. Tori turned and saw Evie first.

"What do you have there?" The pixie flew over. "You know you didn't need to worry about getting us gifts. We love having you here."

"I wanted to give you something more than words as thanks." She held them out. "You've been so kind and generous."

The pixies crowded round, and Tori opened the first

with a flourish. Her hand went to her mouth when she saw the art.

"Oh, Evie, it's beautiful!" She hugged her tightly. "Thank you. We'll cherish them forever."

She gave the others to the two closest pixies who opened them quickly and exclaimed in delight.

"We'll put them up on that wall in pride of place." Samantha gestured excitedly. "They'll be safe from steam and everything over there."

They all hugged Evie and thanked her profusely for her thoughtfulness. Samantha wasted no time and hung the spatulas while Tori guided Evie to her workstation and showed her the recipe they'd work on together that afternoon—a nice tartelette.

"I know you haven't done much savory pastry yet." Tori ran her finger down the recipe. "But don't you worry, your sweet pastries are wonderful. You'll have no trouble with this."

Evie looked at the recipe and was a little concerned about the filling for the pie but was confident she could pull it off. It was a simple French dish with cheesy potatoes and lardons for a filling. It wasn't something she'd eaten before, but her mouth watered at the thought of it.

CHAPTER SEVENTEEN

Raine sat beside Philip at the student council meeting and pursed her lips. She was grateful the wizard had decided that the council fitted his political interests and had been able to take over from another delegate who had chosen to step down.

"I really think a pirate theme would be best." Kerry folded her arms. "It's something we haven't done before."

"This is supposed to be a formal. A pirate theme isn't something you can wear a pretty dress to." Raine refused to budge. "We need something more fitting for the type of dance."

"Well, what about a color theme?" Russ tried not to sigh in frustration. "Something simple and classy—green and gold?"

"That's so tedious." Kerry glared at him. "We need something fun."

"Well, does it have to relate to spring in some way?"

Philip looked at the other students. "Could it perhaps be something more symbolic or literary?"

"What about the 1920s?" Raine was sure she was onto a winner. "With flapper dresses and such?"

The headmistress and Professor Hudson smiled at this. That was a theme they approved of.

Kerry curled her lip, but the rest of the student council were in agreement. The 1920s sounded like a great idea.

"Why don't we refine it and use a Great Gatsby theme?" Russ's mind whirled with ideas. "We could mix in the glitz and glamour with a simple color scheme."

"I love it." The headmistress nodded firmly. "We have agreed on the theme. Now to decide on the actual details."

"A stage at the front could be really cool." Raine could picture it in her mind. "With big crimson-colored curtains behind them and gold ribbons and glitter all around."

"Yes." Philip grinned. "We could add edible glitter and sparkle to the punch and use a black-and-white main theme with splashes of gold to add to the decadence."

"The girls could wear glitzy flapper dresses, and those cool headbands with feathers." Annie gestured excitedly. "And full-length gloves."

"I think the seniors can weave the magic to cover the ceilings and walls. If we produce a facade of pale marble with gold veins and tall pillars, that would be Gatsby-esque I think." Russ looked at Kerry and Annie. "Then, the actual ceiling can have reasonably low-hanging drapes of almost sheer gold over the black and white."

"That sounds perfect to me." Philip made some notes. "I think the freshmen can handle the punch and the edible glitter."

"And the juniors will handle the music." James smiled. "I have an idea for a band that would be cheap, and they should be able to do some appropriate Gatsby music. We can work on the acoustics too. I have some spells in mind."

Raine smiled as everything came together. She and Philip would work with the pixies on the punch and everything relating to that. The others all had their roles and seemed happy with them. Even Kerry began to smile and show some excitement when they talked about the spells they'd use for the walls.

Dances weren't something Raine was usually excited about, but she felt this one had some real potential. She wasn't sure where she'd get a suitable flapper dress, but they had time to work on things like that.

---

Adrien thought about the man who had approached him down in the kemana. It bugged him that the stranger knew who he was and where to find him. If he was honest with himself, what really bugged him was what the wizard had said about his family. He'd told his older brother Etienne who'd shrugged it off as a silly ploy by a jealous family.

Still, the elf had the impression that the man wasn't ready to give up yet. When he received a letter with a crow on the envelope, his suspicions were confirmed.

The letter was short and to the point. The man he had met in the kemana wanted to meet again to properly discuss what he had to say. Adrien had no interest in that. He knew what his family was and did and there wasn't the slightest doubt in his mind as to how much good they did for the world. They had worked long and hard for centuries to protect innocent people from the shadows and ensure their safety and comfort. It was what he himself planned to do with his life.

The elf burned the letter and put the contents of it out of his mind. He returned to his room and looked through the notes he'd made for the history essay he had due in two days. They had gone over the Roswell incident and the real happenings there, along with the impact it had on the human society. He enjoyed history but struggled with that particular topic for some reason. He re-read his notes and tried to focus on what he needed to do.

After a while, Cameron came into the room, shifted into his wolf, and stretched his long legs as he yawned. He'd felt bound by his human form all day and he'd been dying to take a nice nap as a wolf. He was aware of the essays waiting to be written but he'd never be able to focus with the tension and weird muscle itch he got when he needed to shift.

Philip was entirely engrossed in the book he read on business and economics and almost tripped over Cameron when he walked into the room. The shifter looked at him with half-lidded eyes. He stretched, groaned and went back to sleep. Philip sighed and walked around the wolf to his bed.

"He doesn't want wolf fur in his bed." Adrien didn't look up from his books. "This essay seriously isn't happening."

"You need to find the right angle, is all." Philip sat on his bed. "What interests you about the area?"

The elf looked at his notes once more. "Well, I suppose

the impact on the human view of aliens." He picked the top book up. "I find the shift there fascinating."

"Then work the essay around that." Philip shrugged. "She gave us a reasonably broad topic, so we can find our own little niche within it."

Adrien thought it over and finally smiled as the essay began to form in his mind. Finally, the words flowed and he returned to his books to gather relevant citations and quotes.

Cameron returned to his human form when the sun had fully set. He shook his head and stretched his shoulders. The awful itching sensation had left and he could relax again. That meant he had to tackle the mountain of homework he'd avoided. With a sigh, he picked up the first notebook and began looking into the essay on the origin of portals. As much as he might complain outwardly, he enjoyed picking through the information and finding the interesting little snippets here and there.

CHAPTER EIGHTEEN

Raine had gotten side-tracked talking to Professor Fowler about the best books for her to read that week and ran late for her spells class. She jogged down the hallway and tried to sneak into the classroom. Professor Hudson watched her closely with her lips tightly pursed. She didn't say anything as it wasn't like Raine to show up late.

"Today, you will begin with a cleansing spell." The professor glanced at her notes. "These are useful spells to remove any traces of dark magic and help with minor injuries such as cat scratches. Please do remember that more drastic injuries will need stronger treatment such as potions or the aid of a trained healer."

She didn't want to risk one of the students going home and telling their parents she had told them a cleansing spell would replace real healing.

"You will need a clear mind and a calm state with slow,

steady breathing. The aim is to effectively wash the space with your magic."

"Can we use this to do the dishes?" A Light Elf girl asked.

The professor smiled. "No, I'm afraid you'll have to use good old-fashioned elbow grease."

A quiet laugh rippled through the classroom.

"This works best if you can enter a light meditative state first. All the spells we will work on work best with that. You need to calm yourself and clear your mind."

Raine took a slow breath and tried to achieve the required state. She had studied meditation as part of her martial arts, but she hadn't kept up with it. Her mind was prone to run at a mile a minute while she thought of everything she had recently learned.

"We'll begin with that. Take a slow breath and feel yourself calming and relaxing. Your muscles will release their tension and your mind will quieten."

Sara frowned. Her body relaxed but her mind remained full of chatter where she wondered if she could work this spell and how she'd put it to use. Then her mind skipped over to her progress on the painting and which part she'd work on later. Meditation would take a lot of practice.

The professor watched as the students visibly relaxed. She saw a little tension in a couple of them where they clearly couldn't quieten their minds, but it would come with time. After a few minutes of that, she moved on to the spell itself.

"Focus entirely on the item or area you plan to cleanse. Calm your mind and your body, then push your magic around the words 'tabula rasa.' Visualize your magic washing the object clean from the spell."

Raine ran the words through her head and imagined herself performing the spell while the professor placed a small slate in front of each student.

"These slates have a small amount of shadow magic on them. You will perform the spell to remove that shadow magic. Remember, this is a cleansing spell. You can use it to remove the shadow because it makes the slate unclean. It will not work to remove any large amount of shadow. Does that make sense?"

"Yes," the students said.

"Begin when you're ready."

Philip focused on the slate in front of him and lifted his wand slowly. His mind wasn't clear, but he fought to focus through it. He sensed the edges of the smear of shadow and visualized washing it all away with his spell. His magic flowed into his wand, but his mind became busy and offered a hundred different scenarios before he could release the magic. He sighed softly and tried again.

"Stop fighting it." Adrien touched his arm. "You need to allow your mind to empty. The more you try to force it, the more it will fill with thoughts."

The wizard thought about that for a long moment and decided that it made sense in an odd way. He changed his approach and tried to allow his thoughts to slip away from him rather than driving them out. To his delight, it worked. His magic flowed willingly through his wand and he visualized his magic washing the slate. It took him two tries to really clean off the shadow magic, but he was very pleased that he did it.

Raine took her time to calm her mind and felt her magic deep within. The rest of the students were on their second or third attempt when she felt ready to try. She maintained her calm and allowed her magic to stream into her wand before she spoke the words. The shadow magic was erased completely on her first try. She couldn't keep the proud grin from her face. She had worked so hard to really feel and understand her magic. To see it come together filled her with pride and a deep sense of accomplishment.

Evie squeezed her hand. "That was amazing, Raine. Well done!"

"Thank you." She returned the gesture. "I couldn't have made all of this progress without your help. You and the others have been so patient."

Once each student had succeeded in erasing the shadow from their slate, the professor returned to the front of the room.

"Now, we will work on a silence spell. This will form a small bubble of silence around you. It is useful when you need to study or focus on a more complicated working." She pursed her lips and glared at a couple of students with mischievous expressions. "It cannot be cast on others. You cannot silence your friends or rivals, and anyone caught trying to do so will be sent to the headmistress."

Raine was excited by the spell. The library was quiet but there was always a low-level hum of activity and whispers. She looked forward to having absolute silence so she could truly focus on her studies. Although, she realized, she would have to be careful to use it in places where she was entirely safe. It would be far too easy for a potential enemy to sneak up on her if she cast it in the wrong situations.

"I believe Professor Powell has taught you simple bubble shields, yes?"

The students all nodded.

"Good. Then you will use the same visualization while saying *'silentium.'*"

Raine raised her hand.

"How long will the spell last?"

"That depends on how much magic you put into it. There is a natural dimmer switch within the spell. If you infuse a very small amount of magic, it will last only a few minutes. If you pour all your magic into it, then it might last a few days, which might seem blissful to some of you but would, I assure you, cause problems."

Raine nodded, satisfied with that answer. Professor Hudson continued.

"Use only a small thread of magic. We don't need someone in the middle of one of these spells for future classes."

"I don't know, I wouldn't mind skipping portals—"

The professor glared at the young half-elf who had said that.

Raine had mastered the bubble shield spell from Professor Powell and felt reasonably confident working with this silence spell. She summoned her magic and felt it move a little sluggishly into her wand. It was present, but it didn't move as freely as she'd like. She jotted down a note on her notepad to ask Librarian Decker about that later in the library.

Once she had the visualization steady in her mind, she

nudged some of her magic from her wand as she spoke "silentium" clearly.

Suddenly, everything was entirely silent. There wasn't a single sound. She had thought that it would be peaceful and useful for studying, but as she looked around the classroom, she frowned. She didn't feel safe having lost one of her senses. Perhaps it wouldn't be a good study aid after all.

Thankfully, her magic had been sluggish enough that the spell popped after only a minute. Raine looked at the other students as they sat with a look of awe on their faces. Some of them reached out as though they tried to feel the boundary of the silence spell around them. Others frowned and simply waited until they could hear again.

She pursed her lips and considered other potential uses for the spell if it had some minor tweaks. If she could apply it to her feet so they didn't make any sound, that could prove very useful when trying to track down suspects as an agent.

Professor Hudson was satisfied that all the students had succeeded in their casting of the silence spell and ensured that they were all back to their normal state before the class ended. Raine stayed behind at the end as was her habit.

"I'm afraid I don't have any new books for you today." The professor smiled kindly. "Everything I might offer is covered in the books I've already recommended."

"Actually, I wondered if there were other similar spells that might be applied so other people couldn't hear me." Raine frowned. "I mean...is there a spell—or could that spell be tweaked—so I could make it that no one heard me walking? That would be really useful when I track down criminals."

"I will mention you asked after that to Librarian Decker. I'm sure he'll be happy to help you research it. Don't be late to your next class."

"Thank you."

Raine hurried off to join her friends and go to portals class before they were late.

## CHAPTER NINETEEN

Adrien stretched his muscles and tried to focus his mind. This match was the quarter-final in the big championship. The rival team would have already beaten several other teams to get there. They needed to be on their best form so they could progress.

Matt rolled his shoulders and tried to formulate some kind of pep talk. That really wasn't his specialty but he felt like he should say something.

"We're not the oldest team out there." He gestured for the others to gather around. "But we're strong and fast. We're determined. We're going all the way."

Raine took a firebug from Philip and handed the bag to Cameron. She dropped the candy on her tongue and smiled at the warmth that spread through her. The temperature had begun to warm up and it wouldn't be too long before the firebugs wouldn't be necessary anymore.

"Do we know who they're up against?" Sara handed the firebugs along the line. "Is it the Fairbanks Falcons?"

"I think so," Cameron agreed. "I hope the scene they give them isn't anything snowy or cold or they'll have the advantage. I heard their ice magic is ridiculously good up there."

"Damn, that's true. There are many other options, though, where they'll have a more even footing." Philip rearranged his scarf. "Hopefully, there'll be something that can make the most of Adrien and Etienne's combat magic."

"Like the Aztec temple?" William leaned forward as the team walked onto the field. "That would be awesome."

Adrien and Etienne called their swords when the field began to change. The sky was obscured by dark grey rocks overhead. Stalactites grew slowly from the rocks and Adrien sighed. He had never been much of a fan of caves. All that dirt above his head didn't feel right.

The team spread out and examined the space around them. Smaller tunnels led off at the compass points. The main cave they stood in was about the same size as the dining hall with dark grey rock and an almost smooth floor. Orbs of white light danced around them and allowed them to see. Matt sniffed. He caught the scent of running water. There was a stream or river somewhere nearby.

They had four tunnels, and the shifter's instincts were quiet. It was down to luck. He hated that. Etienne took a step toward the southern tunnel. A soft glitter to the floor there had caught his eye.

"Can you see that?" The elf pointed. "The glitter?"

Matt turned and grinned. "Yes, I can. Come on, then. Let's get moving."

They jogged steadily along the southern tunnel. Cody and Daniel kept their wands raised. They were likely to be up against earth-based enemies in this setting. Explosives would be their best chance, much like the Italian village and the golems.

Matt and Etienne took point while Adrien watched everyone's backs. They kept their ears pricked for the sounds of any footsteps or other movement. It was the quarter-final and they knew there would be more obstacles than usual.

The tunnel narrowed slowly and twisted back and forth so they were unable to see very far ahead or behind them. The small lights faded and Daniel and Cody formed their own. Gradually, the once smooth floor became rougher and slowed their pace. Matt grew suspicious at the lack of other places to explore or obstacles to hinder them.

The floor began to crack and crumble beneath their feet and the walls creaked and groaned. The rock around them shifted and reformed into new tunnels, each narrower and shorter than the one they had walked down.

There was no glitter this time. It was down to Matt's instincts to guide them the right way. He took them down the left-hand tunnel as something about it felt right. They had to squeeze between the rock walls which were damp and cold. Adrien didn't like how difficult it was to defend themselves in there. They had absolutely no room to maneuver.

"I couldn't do that." Sara nodded at the cave system. "I'm not a fan of closed spaces and look how close those walls are."

Raine had been more concerned with how difficult it was to move in there. The team would come up against either the rival team or some form of obstacle and they wouldn't have a chance in that tight tunnel. She desperately wanted to widen it for them and give them better odds.

After what felt like an age, the players emerged from the tunnel into a honeycomb of interconnected caves. Cody drew a deep breath and smiled, glad to have open air around him again. Of course, they knew it was some form of trap. They remained at the very edge of the cavern and looked for some sign of what to do or where to go.

Small symbols glistened like oil against the dark stone. Matt frowned at them. He recognized them from history class, but he couldn't place them. Etienne's mouth thinned.

"We jump from the slender triangular one to the dual lines, back and forth. Don't touch the others."

The sound of footsteps echoed around them. Someone or something drew closer. They began to jump onto the flat spaces with the relevant symbols. It took every ounce of balance the wizards had to stay upright, and Matt made a note to himself to include balance training in their next session. As a shifter, he had no difficulty, and the elves had trained for many years in similar things.

Once they were all safe and stood in front of a smaller cave which had an eerie green glow to it, the guardian appeared. Where they had expected a rock being or something similar, they instead saw a small, thin man dressed in ridiculous wizards' attire. His long robe was almost black with hand-stitched stars, and his pointed hat had a crick at the very tip.

The elves drew their swords and the wizards formed fireballs. Matt stepped aside and looked for a way through the cave. The ground didn't look stable—it bobbed ever so slightly as though it rested on water. The wizard took a step forward and the slab of rock beneath his feet sank a little, confirming the captain's suspicions. He thought it was likely a speed test, which was something they'd trained intensely for.

While the others threw fireballs and explosive spells at the wizard, who had a very effective shield, Matt edged around the room and searched for a hint as to where to go next. Then he saw a pale golden glow in the northern-most cave. The token had to be in there.

Footsteps thundered around them, but no one saw the source. Shadows stretched along the walls and finally, Matt realized that the wall to his left wasn't rock like the others. It was a large window. The rival team faced a classic witch with a large hooked nose and pale green skin.

Adrien delivered the final blow to the wizard, an explosive spell that knocked his absurd hat off before he vanished.

"We need to run fast and stay close together." Matt pointed to the cave with the golden glow. "That's our goal."

Everyone nodded as the witch pushed the rival team back into the tunnel. They had the advantage if they could run quickly enough. Matt raced across the rough floor and felt the pieces of rock move beneath his feet. Adrien brought up the rear and caught Cody when he tripped. The elf grabbed the back of his shirt and threw him bodily forward before his feet could sink into the black water beneath the stone.

The wizard caught himself and continued to run with everything he had. Adrien leapt from the sinking stone and landed on the hard ground with a victorious grin. They'd all made it.

Matt didn't hesitate for even a moment. They rushed into the cave with the glow and Daniel sighed softly when he saw the token perched at the top of a large column of stone. Hand grips were hewn in the rough rock, but it wasn't an easy climb.

"Adrien, come with me. The rest of you, watch our backs," Matt ordered

The elf threw himself at the stone column and climbed with the confidence that came with years of experience. As he got higher, the handholds became sparser and his muscles began to complain. The gold token was within sight, however, and he wouldn't give up.

He dug deep and pushed himself to stretch for the crevices and haul himself upward. The column shook when he was only a few feet away. He decided to climb more quickly and take the risk rather than attempt to grip on and ride it out. With one final push, he dragged himself over the top lip and lifted the token.

Raine stood up and cheered for the team. They had fought hard and she was so pleased to see all their hard work and training pay off. The Cardinals were one step closer to the big championship.

# CHAPTER TWENTY

The spring formal dance was only a few days away, and the girls needed to get their dresses. Sara kept watch while Evie and Raine put their stealth spells in place. Once they were done, she wrapped hers around her quickly and they ducked behind a group of seniors and ran down to the kemana. She couldn't hold back her laugh of glee as they hurried down the main walkway toward the cluster of clothing shops. They slowed their pace once they were sufficiently out of view of the stairs.

"We need flapper dresses." Sara hooked her arms through Evie and Raine's. "And those cute little headdress thingies they used to wear."

Uncle Jerry had sent Raine a little extra money for her to buy a nice dress for the dance. She was excited to explore what they had on offer in the kemana. They turned a corner and stepped into the clothing district. There were other stores there too— shoes, perfumes, and jewelry—but most were clothing stores.

The girls walked past several very modern stores selling jeans, t-shirts, and other day-to-day clothes. They wanted something a little more specific and Sara spotted it first. She pointed enthusiastically to the window that stretched the length of two shops. On display within were a few extravagant gowns and dresses. Sara studied the details of a red dress with a large skirt and a number of ruffles with faux rubies at the apex of each ruffle.

"I don't think that'll fit with the theme." Evie guided Sara into the shop. "But this is the best possibility we've seen so far."

The girls looked around the room which appeared to be split into styles. The area nearest the large display window was full of large, almost wedding-style dresses with big skirts and an abundance of ruffles and taffeta. Raine ignored that entirely. She had no interest in any dress with a large skirt. She made her way to the flapper-style dresses tucked into the east corner.

Sara held up a black dress with a straight neckline and a long fringe that put the hem just below her knee. Delicate black and silver beads had been sewn into a broad diamond pattern. The dress itself seemed loose fitting, but when Sara put it on, it hugged her figure in the right ways. She made a quick spin with a huge grin on her face.

"It's perfect." Evie's hand went to her mouth. "You have to get it."

"I agree. That is stunning. You look incredible," Raine said warmly. "You'll take it, right?"

"Oh, I need to find shoes and the little headdress." Sara looked around. "I think the shop across the way might have shoes."

She went to change into her normal clothes while Evie and Raine looked through the rest of the dresses. Evie held up a dark silver dress, but she didn't like how low the neckline fell.

"What do you think? I'm not sure."

"I don't think that's your color." Raine glanced at the rack but saw nothing better. "There are other shops."

Sara had a bounce in her step as she carried the paper bag with her dress into the third shoe store. Evie had found her perfect shoes in the first store—a pair of low-heeled black shoes with glitter on the toes. Raine waited to find her dress before she settled on her shoes. She didn't want to fall in love with a beautiful pair of shoes only to not find a dress to go with them.

They stopped at a stall selling hot dogs and gyros which the girls ate with relish.

"How are these so good?" Evie finished her hot dog. "I've been to both New York and Chicago and these beat those."

"They're amazing." Sara wiped her hands. "We'll have to show it to the guys."

Raine took her time finishing her gyro. The chicken had been nicely spiced and the pita bread was warm and fresh. They were something she'd first tasted when she'd visited Germany with her uncle. They weren't all that easy to find where she'd grown up, but she enjoyed eating them when she could.

Once the girls were ready to return to shopping, they headed into a small boutique and were about to walk out again when Raine spotted a small hallway. This led them into a room full of old-fashioned party dresses complete with the accouterments. Sara immediately went to the accessories while the other two girls looked through the dresses.

Raine fell in love with a dark blue dress with black sequins sewn in a complicated pattern that included flowers on the skirt. The black fringe fell a couple of inches below her knees and the neckline was just below her collarbone. She looked herself up and down in the mirror and felt happy. The dress was far better than she'd hoped to find.

Evie found a stunning pale-silver dress with layers of fringe and a simple matching headband with a thin line of sequins along the center. Sara insisted that Raine needed a black headband with three feathers sticking up from above her right ear. She had to admit that it did pair very well with her dress.

The girls walked out with everything they needed for the dance. Raine checked her watch and realized they had ten minutes to get back to school. They ran down the streets and ducked and twisted around groups of witches and a pair of Kilomea. A Willen stepped out in front of Sara but she dodged around her and ran for the stairs. They made quick work of their stealth spells and ran up the stairs, across the grounds, and into the school.

Professor Fowler stood near the stairs with a thoughtful expression on her face. The girls slowed and tried to look inconspicuous as they sauntered past her. Sara laughed and leaned back against the wall as the adrenaline flooded her system.

"Well, we cut that a bit close."

Raine had talked her friends into joining her for the freshmen's' part in the dance preparations. They were in charge of the punch and decorations relating to that. Professor Fowler stood at the front of the classroom with a potion recipe written on the board behind her.

"This will make the punch look like liquid gold. It won't affect the taste and has no side-effects. It's purely aesthetic."

"This is so cool." Sara grinned. "I definitely need to do this for parties back at home."

Raine added the gold glitter and pyrite dust into the icy cold water. She stirred four times clockwise and three times counter-clockwise. Evie helped her with the next stage where they had to bring the water up to a gentle simmer.

Evie added in the daisy petals and Raine stirred in a slow, methodical fashion, making sure that the potion didn't thicken too quickly. After another fifteen minutes and a few more petals, they had enough vials of the potion to make a couple of gallons of punch look like liquid gold. Professor Fowler ensured that every batch was perfect and entirely safe for the students.

Once these were complete, they moved onto working with Professor Hudson to add layers of glitter and sparkle to the glasses. They produced a visual spell that would require far less clean-up the following day. No one wanted to spend the next three months finding glitter everywhere.

Raine frowned as she struggled to form her magic in the delicate way that was required for the spells. After a few attempts, she excused herself and left to help the sophomores with the balloons and ribbons around the tables and the stage. A tall, dark-haired wizard showed her how to form the air spell that filled the balloons much more quickly. Raine was pleased that she picked that one up quickly and enjoyed seeing the dining hall transformed around her.

She could see that when everyone was finished, it would be spectacular. The other students would be very pleased with their efforts.

# CHAPTER TWENTY-ONE

"Oh, wow, you all look gorgeous. Your dresses are so beautiful. Do you want me to help with some make-up? I have some spells and lotions that will really make you shine. Sara, that headband is perfect. Where did you find it all? I had to have mine shipped over from London. My mum was good about it. She knows all the best boutiques and I didn't have time to go down into the kemana. Did I tell you that I'm learning the violin now? As well as the piano and flute—I'm in the orchestra with my flute. Then there's choir, and I'm in the musical too. We're doing Cats this year. You'll come and watch, won't you?"

Raine smoothed her dress down and smiled at Christie as she waited to be sure she had finished talking.

"Of course we'll be there for the musical. And thank you, we got lucky with the dresses. You look stunning, Christie, really—that shade of green brings out your eyes." Raine glanced in the mirror. "I'd love to see what magical help you have for make-up. It's not my strongest area."

"Sit. I'll get everything."

Raine sat in front of the mirror and Christie brought over an armful of jars, vials, and small bottles. She raised an eyebrow at the sheer number of products their roommate appeared to have.

"I've been experimenting. This should add a pretty sheen to your hair." Christie picked up a small silver jar. "I'll start with that and we can move onto your face. I have an eyeshadow that shines like burnished metal. I think this gunmetal-colored one will really make your eyes pop."

She stroked sections of her hair gently to create shimmery highlights that brought out her cheekbones and made Raine smile. She watched her transformation with fascination. Christie moved on to apply a cool creamy colored foundation to her skin before she added the next layers. She finished with the eyeshadow she'd mentioned. Raine opened her eyes and laughed. She almost didn't recognize herself in the mirror. Her eyes really did pop as promised, and she looked more mature and elegant.

"Wow, thank you so much, Christie."

"It's what friends are for."

Sara was next in the make-up chair. Christie had a fine powder that made her hair look as though it flickered with soft flames and her eyes looked like bright emeralds. Sara grinned at her reflection and stood to spin around in her dress. She felt on top of the world. Once Christie had finished, the girls all sparkled and glimmered and felt like princesses. Raine had never been all that interested in dances before, but this one felt magical in the best possible ways. She was excited to see how the dining hall had been transformed and the students' reactions to the liquid-gold punch.

Christie left to be with her own friends. Raine and the others went to meet the guys at the top of the broad staircase. They had all dressed in suits with vests beneath. Philip's pinstripe suit had been paired with a black-and-cream striped tie and a hat. He grinned at the girls.

"Wow, you look incredible." Cameron walked up to Raine. "You're absolutely stunning. I mean, you're always beautiful, but wow."

She blushed and smiled. "Thanks, you look really good too." The shifter wore a pitch-black suit with a navy-blue silk vest. "I wasn't sure you'd ever wear a suit."

He shrugged with a smile. "I like to be prepared for every occasion." He held out his arm for Raine to take. "May I have the honor of taking you to this dance?"

"I would love to—I mean, yes." Raine hooked her arm through his and moved closer to his side. "I'm excited about this dance."

"Me too." Sara couldn't keep the huge grin off her face. "You did amazing work with the theme."

William put his hands in the pockets of his pants and looked bashfully at Evie. "Would you be my date to the dance?" He looked away. "I know I should have asked sooner."

Evie walked over to the nervous half-Ifrit and looped her arm around his. "I had planned to ask you myself."

Sara moved to stand between Philip and Adrien.

"It looks like you guys are all mine." She grinned at them. "I'm sure we'll survive."

The elf laughed and put his arm out for Sara to take. Philip mirrored the gesture and the friends walked down the staircase toward the dining hall. Students flowed along the hallways in front of them in all their finery. The girls wore glittery and sequined dresses in the typical flapper style. Many had small feathers and some had pearls or diamante in drop designs or large feathers. Everyone looked incredibly glamorous. The guys all wore traditional suits, some in pinstripes and others in something a little easier to wear again.

The music and a rich voice like that of Frank Sinatra filled the hallway and broadened Raine's smile. She hadn't listened to much music from that era but she had done a little research into it. She enjoyed the energy it had and the strength of Sinatra's beautiful voice made her want to get onto the dance floor.

The dining hall had been transformed into a glitzy dance hall with white marble floors complete with gold veins, and a thick layer of black and gold balloons covered the tall ceiling overhead. Ribbons had been tied around the edges of the small round tables that clustered on the left side of the room. Black tablecloths allowed the tables to almost blend in and maintain the focus on the dance floor where the students all laughed and danced, thoroughly enjoying themselves. Raine saw looks of awe and glee on the students' faces at the liquid-gold-looking punch.

"We have to try some." Sara tugged on Adrien's arm. "We helped make it, but we never got to taste it."

Adrien went along with Sara good-naturedly and scooped some of the punch into a heavily glittered champagne flute. The effect was memorable. The glitter of the spell around the glass added depth to the gold of the punch and made it look like pure decadence. Sara took a sip and her hand flew to her mouth.

"Wow, that is incredible." She pointed to the bowl. "You guys have to try some."

Cameron poured a glass for Raine and the group formed a small circle away from the bowl so they weren't in the way.

"To friendships, happiness, and continued progress." Philip held his glass up. "Together, we'll change the world."

They clinked their glasses and took a sip. Raine was surprised by the layers of flavor in the punch. Blueberries exploded on her tongue, quickly chased by strawberries dipped in honey, and finally, it finished with soft elderflower. She knew there was some magic involved, but she'd still never dreamed it would taste that good.

Sara took Adrien and Philip onto the dance floor where they danced to the live band. Raine absorbed more of the smaller details the older students had added to the decorations. The bold red velvet curtain hung behind the semicircular stage where the band played. A taller Light Elf tapped his foot to the beat he played on the double bass while the slender wizard sang with heart and soul.

Once Raine had finished her punch, Cameron held his arm out and pointed toward the dance floor. "Would you like to dance?"

She hadn't seen this gentler, quiet side of the shifter before and wasn't sure what to make of it although she thoroughly enjoyed his company. A slower song started, and he placed one hand lightly on her hip and took her hand in the other. They danced a simple slow dance as neither of them was quite sure how to do something more complicated.

"Your eyes are shining tonight. I've seen them do that when you find a particularly fascinating topic to study in the library." Cameron smiled gently. "I don't mean that to be creepy. I just think you're incredible. You're so passionate and dedicated."

Raine blushed. She enjoyed his company, but she'd been too wrapped up in school to think of him as anything more than a friend. His thumb brushed over hers and she moved a little closer to him.

"Thank you." She wasn't sure what to say. This was all new to her. "You're pretty amazing yourself."

Cameron preened under the praise and guided her slowly around the dance floor as the next song—something more upbeat—started. They wove their way around the other pairs dancing in a steady circle. Sara, Adrien, and Philip had somehow ended up at the center of the circle and were having a fantastic time. Raine danced without a care in the world and felt the weight of everything lifted from her shoulders. There were only the music and the happiness at being surrounded by her friends.

Evie and William sat at a small table and watched everyone else on the dance floor. She put her hand on his and smiled gently. "I admire you." Evie squeezed his hand. "You had a bad start in life but you're determined to make something really good come of it. You work so hard, and you always try to find a positive spin."

The half-Ifrit blushed and looked away. He had liked

Evie for a while, but he'd never had the confidence to do or say anything about it. "You're the kindest, most beautiful person I've ever met. I'm lucky to call you my friend."

Evie wasn't entirely sure what to say from there, so she scooted her chair closer to his and leaned against him as they watched the students dancing. She was content to enjoy the music and be close to him.

After a few songs, William finally plucked up the courage to ask her to dance. The final slow song came on and she was happy to accompany him onto the dance floor where they swayed together with his hands on her sides and hers on his shoulders. Raine and Cameron danced near them with contented smiles on both of their faces. Sara still danced with both Adrien and Philip. They laughed at an inside joke while they danced in a triangle.

Sara saw the way Evie and Raine had paired off and she was happy for them. She was also glad no one had asked her to dance like that as she wasn't ready to think of anyone like that. Sara was happy to laugh and dance with Adrien and Philip purely as friends without any complications. Still, she quietly hoped that Evie and Raine became more than friends with their respective dance partners. She wanted her friends to be happy and they were so very happy around each other.

When the final song was finished, the group went to a quiet hallway at the back of the building where the window sills were wide enough to sit on.

"That was amazing." Sara leaned back against the wall and tucked her legs under her. "And the best part is that there'll be barely any clean-up tomorrow as most of it was magic."

"Magic definitely has some awesome advantages." Evie leaned against William. "I'm so glad to not have to try to clean glitter up from everywhere."

"That theme was genius." Philip grinned at Raine. "Well done."

"It seems to have been a hit. I didn't hear any complaints." Raine smiled as Cameron entwined his fingers with hers. "Although I'm not looking forward to figuring out the theme for the next dance. It's so much harder than it sounds"

---

"You were a vision tonight." Xander took Mara's hand in his own. "I don't believe I've seen you smile like that in a number of years."

She gazed at the clear night sky where the stars glistened like diamonds set in pitch silk.

"Everything came together beautifully. There were no incidents, and I have always enjoyed that music." She looked at him. "I'm so pleased to see you back to yourself. I missed seeing that spark in your eyes."

He stepped a little closer as a look of mischief settled on his face.

Mara laughed and began walking across the grounds toward their cottages. She allowed Xander to hold her hand, but she wasn't ready for the affection he had in mind.

"Things seem to finally be quieting and settling." He allowed himself a peaceful smile. "As much as I enjoyed the excitement in my younger years, I'm glad to have peace now."

Mara shook her head. "Don't give me that, Xander Powell." She smirked at him. "You'll be an adventurer and hero until the day you die."

He laughed. "Well, when you put it like that…"

# CHAPTER TWENTY-TWO

"What are we watching tonight?" William opened the door to the movie room for Evie and Raine. "Another zombie movie, right?"

"*Day of the Dead.*" Evie walked into the room. "It's a bit more modern than the other movies, but I think it's still cheesy enough."

"And the zombies are more like we're used to." Raine gave Cameron and Philip a small wave. "At least I think they are. I've only seen images here and there."

Everyone settled into their favorite seat and William popped the popcorn. Raine passed the second pack of Twizzlers to Evie and Sara added M&Ms into her popcorn. Philip hit play on the movie and they all focused on the screen.

"Well, this music is very eighties," Sara commented. "It has a very different aesthetic feel to the movies from the sixties that we watched."

"Has anyone seen the modern version of this?" Adrien

stretched his legs out in front of him. "They remade it a few years ago, I think."

"I'm not a big fan of remakes," Philip responded. "Sometimes, they can be cool, but I don't know. It's nice to keep the originals, you know?"

"I think it partially depends on how long they wait before they do a remake," Evie reasoned. "If it's done within a decade, it can feel like a cash grab, but if it's a couple of decades, then it's being remade for a whole new generation."

They watched as the camera focused on a skeleton and cash blown down the street by a harsh wind.

"Oh, wow, they really went to town with that zombie." Sara put a handful of popcorn into her mouth. "The special effects still aren't up to modern standards, but it's far closer to what we think of than the last movie. He even has that classic zombie groan down."

"Why was that zombie dragging a basket behind it?" Cameron frowned. "I mean, zombies are driven by a desire to eat, right? Isn't that the theory? That they have nothing but the need to eat. Carrying a basket around doesn't make any sense."

"This comes back to the discussion on how much sentience they have left," Philip stated. "But I agree, dragging a basket behind them is definitely weird."

"At least they have the sense to have good fences and a secure place to hide out," Cameron said. "I think that's something that would catch most people out in a zombie apocalypse."

"I think you're right. Most people will panic and run out of food which will lead to mistakes. There was a study showing that being out in the middle of nowhere was the best place for the first couple of months." Raine took a bite of her Twizzler. "But after that, it was more dangerous to be out there because the zombies migrate out of the cities when they run out of food."

"Surely it comes down to being able to wait them out?" He offered Raine some of his popcorn. "I mean, they'll rot and fall apart right?"

"I guess that depends on the details of the zombie virus. The fact that they can move without a beating heart goes against nature, to begin with." Raine traded Cameron a Twizzler for a handful of his popcorn. "Given that you're starting from a base that doesn't exist in a world we know, we can't really be sure what would happen."

"And you have to take into consideration whether they're scientific zombies or necromancer zombies," William pointed out as he pulled his blanket over his lap. "Necromancer zombies will have magic running through them, which means they can be guided and potentially have more sentience. It'd also affect the degradation of their bodies."

"Necromancers are a terrifying thought." Sara wrinkled her nose. "I hope they don't exist. I really don't want to bump into a zombie at any point."

"Dark wizards play with anything they feel they can use to their advantage." Adrien sighed. "I'm sure zombies have wandered around somewhere thanks to one of them."

"Why do they always feel the need to have a pet zombie or at least a zombie in a cage?" Cameron asked. "The risk isn't worth the reward."

"I can understand it in a scientific facility where

they're trying to find a cure," Raine ventured. "But in this situation where it's a military base? I guess maybe the zombie was someone they cared about, but I'd have thought that seeing them in zombie form would only make it worse."

"Why is she shooting from the hip?" Adrien sighed again. "She's supposed to be military trained and should know how to handle a gun."

"It's a weird thing that movies do." Philip shrugged. "Maybe they think it looks more badass?"

The movie showed a laboratory deep underground with rock walls and bloody rags strewn around.

"That's not even close to sanitary or suitable for lab work," Sara muttered in distaste. "How can he call himself a doctor when he works in such unsterile conditions?"

"If the core is the last to go, it makes sense to have the instincts remain intact, but surely their motor functions would vanish?" Cameron frowned as he considered this. "This says that they do rot, but it also makes sense that they would collapse somewhere and slowly die from starvation. And speaking of starvation, how does that even work? The eating, I mean. We've established that their heart doesn't work so why do they eat? And how does it keep their body functioning? Normal humans can't only eat meat like that. It damages the body."

"It's an ancient myth. I don't think it entirely makes sense." Raine shrugged. "Like dragons. Look at the size of them. The amount of prey they'd need to live let alone maintain a breeding population is insane. Then you think about the number of dragons needed within the population to stop inbreeding from causing major issues and it becomes very implausible. And yet, dragons are present in myths around the world."

"Aren't zombies actually more closely tied to witches and such?" William asked. "Not our type of witches, but the ones the humans think of. I know one type of zombies come from the use of poison from the...I've forgotten. One of those poisonous fish. It paralyzes the person and they use another poison to bring them partially back but with limits on their brain functioning so they're easy to manipulate."

"I think so, but that poison didn't spread all around the world. It could be a generalized fear of death." Raine ate a piece of her Twizzler. "And they could have been mixed up with vampires too. The original vampires were horrifying and far closer to zombies. They were haggard, rotting, and so on."

"That's true." Cameron smiled. "You're really something, Raine, you know that?"

She smiled, unsure what to say to that.

They were halfway through the film when she said, "Why must they insist on trying to domesticate the zombies? This is something else they keep trying to do in the movies."

"Well, they're pain resistant, strong, and so on," Adrien explained. "They could have military uses if they were truly domesticated."

Raine shook her head. "They're also highly contagious and require human flesh to exist. The risk is so ridiculous. I fail to see how the positives could possibly outweigh the negatives."

"I agree." Evie nodded. "Look, the scientist is telling

everyone to go in with the domestic zombie. They'll all get eaten, and frankly, they deserve it. They shouldn't play with things like that anyway."

"It must be weird to act as one of those zombies," William muttered. "And it'd have to hurt your throat with those weird throaty groans and things he does."

"Oh, that's great, they gave the zombie a gun." Philip shook his head. "That's just what this situation needs. Zombies that know how to use and have access to guns."

Everyone laughed.

"It's like they're trying to get themselves killed," Sara said and laughed. "They have a great situation. A safe bunker, clean water, and vehicles that give them access to more food when they need it. They simply have to ride it out."

"That scientist is so accurate, though," Cameron pointed out. "People can't resist playing. They need to poke, prod, and experiment. The idea of playing God, of seeing how far they can go, is an inherent part of human nature."

"I suppose everything has to have its flaws," Raine said thoughtfully. "I hope that people do at least learn something from the books and movies. There are so many forms of apocalypse that have been predicted. We can avoid them if people listen to the art."

"I'm hoping for a robot apocalypse myself." Philip grinned. "I feel as though robots wouldn't be so bad as long as you left them alone."

"I don't know. Skynet wasn't exactly friendly," William reminded him. "They did put reasonable effort into trying to wipe humans out."

"I never understood why, though," Evie interjected.

"Personally, I hope it's more like *iRobot* where they get really protective over humans."

"Would that count as an apocalypse in that case?" William asked her. "Sure, it wouldn't be as cozy as we might like, but is it strictly an apocalypse if they're keeping us safe?"

"I think there's an argument to be made for it becoming more of a dystopia." Philip placed his empty popcorn bag down. "Not as grim as some other options, but still a dystopia."

"At what point does it become a dystopia?" Raine wondered. "I mean, where is the line that everything becomes bad enough that it's a dystopia? If the robots kept us safe and comfortable, then can we really call it that? It might not be as we would prefer, but as long as we're cared for, it can't really cross that line."

"It depends on how far the robots go to protect us." Philip thought for a moment. "They could go far enough that it did become deeply unpleasant for us. If they decided that we didn't truly need freedom, for example, we could end up living in small boxes with the appropriate amount of nutrition and such. That would satisfy our biological needs if not our social ones."

"And that's a key part of it. How much of an understanding of humans do these robots have?" Cameron spread his hands wide. "If they have only been programmed with a basic understanding, then they might inadvertently harm us despite having good intentions."

"Ah, but so many dystopias start with the very best of intentions," Philip added. "Many of them begin with a government drive to protect and safeguard the people, except they take it to an extreme."

"And therein lies the problem." Cameron smiled. "Extremes are bad, in any and every direction. Balance is always the best solution and results in the most pleasant situation."

"Unfortunately, humans love taking things to the extreme." Evie sighed. "They—we—have such curiosity that we must know how everything works and what happens if we press that big red button."

"But that is why people like us go into positions like the FBI and government. To provide an anchor and balance to those who have stronger curiosity and a need to push to extremes." Raine gestured at the group. "It's down to people like us to help make sure that things exist as they need to and no one can go too far."

"It is down to us to protect those who cannot protect themselves," Adrien affirmed. "And it is also down to us to watch over each other and balance each other."

"Perfectly put." Philip patted the elf on the back. "You said exactly what we were getting at."

"On the topic of the movie..." Sara pointed to the scene with the domestic zombie and the scientist. "How is it that zombies, and for that matter, vampires, are always stronger than people? That makes absolutely no sense."

"I think there's a theory to do with the oxygen uptake for vampires," William suggested. "That's supposed to explain why they're faster too. Although, if you're talking the vampires that can turn into a mist or bats, then there's clearly magic involved."

"Honestly, I think people make zombies stronger

because it makes them scarier." Philip shrugged. "If you could easily beat them off, they wouldn't be very scary."

"See." Cameron pointed to the scene where the military guys turned on the scientist. "That's why zombies could never work in the military. How could you expect people to work closely alongside something like that? Something that needs to eat human flesh to continue existing?"

"I liked *Shaun of the Dead's* approach." Sara grinned. "At the very end where he plays on the games console with his zombified friend."

"Yes," William agreed. "That movie was awesome. It's like Shrek. It revolutionized things and brought a fresh angle to the genre."

"Dude, Shrek was and still is amazing," Sara enthused. "I've seen it so many times I'm pretty sure I can recite the entire script and I still love it."

They finished the movie without much more commentary.

"I expected far more zombies," Sara said as she helped Evie put the blankets away. "It seems like the modern movies are where they really brought in a more zombie focus."

"I think zombie movies always focus on the people stuck in the close confines." Cameron gathered up the empty root beer bottles. "That's a lot of their purpose and artistry."

"Too much thinking for me." Sara laughed. "I'd rather laugh at goofy monsters."

"I agree." Raine handed Philip her trash. "I enjoy movies where I can relax and simply watch. I do so much thinking through the day, it's nice to not think for a little while."

"There's something to be said for movies that allow you to do that," Cameron agreed. "It's far more difficult than people give it credit for."

"And they have far more value in society than people would say too." Evie opened the door to leave. "We need those breaks, those moments of pure light entertainment. It's good for us."

They all filtered out of the room and Adrien placed the spells back over the door. He always came away from the movie nights feeling invigorated and happy to have such fantastic friends.

# CHAPTER TWENTY-THREE

"Have you seen my history homework?" William stripped his bed in his frantic search. "I finished it last night and I can't find it now. My laptop screwed up and I don't have a saved copy."

"Did you eat it?" Adrien grinned at Cameron.

The shifter laughed heartily. "It's not to my taste. Now, if your homework had been a steak..."

The half-Ifrit dragged his fingers through his hair. He'd pulled his part of the room apart and been through every-thing—he'd even checked under his mattress and in his pillowcases. There was no sign of it.

Cameron walked over to him and put his hands on his upper arms. "Breathe." The shifter held his gaze. "We'll help you do it again. We have this afternoon."

Philip patted William on the back. "Don't worry. We'll have you all sorted out in no time." He pulled out the history books he'd borrowed from the library. "I don't need to return these until tomorrow."

Adrien handed William a notebook and pen.

"Come and sit down. We'll figure it out together." He guided him to the small desk they all shared. "Now, what was your topic?"

"The Oriceran impact on Mayan mythology." William settled himself into the chair. "I think I remember half of it."

"That's great." Philip grinned and picked up the top book. "I think I know the section on the Mayan stuff."

"We'll head down to the library and pick up a couple more books." Cameron looked at Adrien. "I'm sure Raine will have some suggestions too."

The half-Ifrit began to relax. "You guys are the best." He opened his laptop and wrote the title. "I don't know what I'd do without you."

Philip pulled up a chair beside him and helped him find the relevant parts in the books they already had. "Do you want me to help with the essay itself?" He handed him the book, open at the relevant section. "Or I can pull out references and citations for you."

"I'm not great at structuring essays so I'd appreciate some help on that." William skimmed the book. "This is perfect, thank you."

Cameron was pleased to see Raine in her usual spot in the library. He smiled when he saw a strand of hair fall into her face as she read a book she was entirely engrossed in. The shifter sat beside her and waited for her to notice him. He loved the deep pleasure in her eyes when she studied. She was never happier than when she was in the library learning something new.

"Oh, hey, Cameron." Raine looked at him with a bright smile. "I didn't expect to see you until dinner."

"Ah, well, William's laptop ate his history essay." He put his elbows on the table. "Is there any chance you could help us find some relevant books for him?"

"Oh, I'd love to." She tidied the table. "What topic are we looking for?"

"The Oriceran impact on Mayan myths."

"That's such a good topic." Raine stood. "I'm jealous."

Cameron followed her through the aisles of books and stood a little closer than was necessary when they stopped at the right shelves.

"I think these three will be best." She handed him the books. "I'm already at my limit for borrowed books, so they'll have to be under your name."

"Not a problem. We'll return them all tonight anyway." Cameron looked at them and found he didn't have an excuse to stick around anymore. "I'll see you at dinner."

Raine watched him leave and sighed. She wanted to spend more time with him and really get to know him, but she didn't know how to initiate that. Also, she had very little spare time. She'd studied the warding spell they'd covered the day before. It was a more complicated spell that worked to cleanse the area of any non-useful magic while it contained whatever magic was brought into the space. It was used during more complicated rituals and workings. She had thought that it would be very useful for a more complicated tracking spell that would be great when she was hunting down criminals.

The warding spell, however, proved more difficult than Raine had anticipated. She had read up on the various methods and purposes for the spell for two hours. Still, something hadn't quite clicked in her mind. She understood that it was like a bubble shield at its core in that it formed a sort of bubble of cleansing and protection. The difference was that it held magic in rather than focused on keeping magic out. Other forms of it did both, but they were even more complicated and she wasn't ready to investigate those yet.

Head Librarian Decker approached her when he heard her sigh and saw her frown at the books. He had seen Raine in the library enough times to know it meant she had difficulty with something. The other gnomes were perfectly capable of watching over things and he wanted to help her. She put her heart and soul into everything and he didn't like seeing her struggle.

"Is there anything I can help with?" He ignored his poppy which blew raspberries. "You look like you're stuck."

"Well, I'm trying to master this warding spell and I can't quite grasp it." Raine pointed to the book in front of her. "I know the principles, but I can't make my magic flow the way it needs to. It seems to hit a dam after the first rune."

The head librarian frowned and looked at the spell in question. It was one he himself had used many times over the years. "Why don't you show me and I'll see what's going wrong?"

Raine smiled and visibly relaxed. She stood and placed the runes she'd written onto separate sheets of paper onto the floor around her in a neat circle. The runes were all drawn with exact precision, so he knew there wasn't a problem there. She lifted her wand and pointed at the first one.

He said nothing but could already see where she went wrong. He was sure that the professor had told them to point at the runes in turn to push the magic into them as that helped them visualize the spell flowing. Unfortunately, it also led to the students pressing too hard on an individual rune if they were a perfectionist like Raine.

Librarian Decker watched and nodded to himself as he saw Raine push her magic into the rune, but she tensed as she did so. Her magic sputtered and died before it flowed into the next. He smiled in a fatherly way.

"I recommend you approach this in a different manner to what your professor taught you." He rolled his shoulders. "Currently, you focus on each one at a time, correct?"

"Yes." Raine looked at the runes. "Is that wrong?"

"Not strictly, no. It makes visualization easier." He smiled. "However, some students are perfectionists and become stuck on a rune, which I believe is what's happening here. I recommend that you close your eyes and visualize the completed spell. You should see a web of violet magic connecting each rune. From that web, a pale-blue bubble will rise and close above your head."

Raine frowned as she pulled the image together in her head. She turned slowly and looked at each rune to solidify their image in her mind before she looked at the next. Then, she looked at them as a group and visualized how the web would connect them. When she was ready, she lifted her wand, closed her eyes, and pushed her magic into the combined image in her mind.

Her magic was stubborn and spluttered from the end of her wand. She knew from the head librarian's previous lessons that it meant she fought too hard with it and needed to relax and let it flow. After taking a deep breath and exhaling through her nose, Raine tried again. She slowed her breathing and tried to get out of the way of her magic while maintaining the complicated image in her mind.

Librarian Decker watched as the spell slowly unfurled and came together. A swell of pride filled him as the web formed and the bubble clicked into place over her head. She was one of the hardest working people he'd ever met, and she never failed him. Sometimes, she simply needed a little help to view things from a fresh angle.

Raine grinned. She could see and feel the spell in place. It had worked beautifully and the web and bubble were entirely flawless. The spell had taken longer than she would have liked, but she'd done it through hard work and dedication.

"Thank you so much, Librarian Decker. As always, you have been a wonderful teacher and for that, I am grateful."

# CHAPTER TWENTY-FOUR

Sara applied the final stroke to the landscape painting she'd worked on for Professor Powell. She smiled and felt incredibly proud of how well it had come together. It had taken longer than she had initially told the professor, but she felt the extra little details were worth it. She had added a light touch of her magical paints that added depth and made the trees around the base of the mountains pop and come to life.

It would take another day to dry completely and be safe to transport, but the professor would arrive in a few minutes. He wanted to see the final piece and pick out a suitable frame for it. She couldn't hold back her glee at the thought of having one of her paintings framed. It was something she'd dreamed of and worked toward, and it was really happening. She was one step closer to having her pieces in a gallery. Sara wasn't sure how her painting would go once she began training to be a lawyer, but she hoped to be able to do a couple of pieces a year, for herself if nothing else.

That meant she savored the time and space she had while she was in school. She had experimented with new paints and techniques to create art that she was proud of. It was exciting, and she felt that she had come into her own and found her individual style.

Professor Powell walked into the room and stopped when he saw the painting. His face slowly lit up with joy as he took in the details of the art and walked closer to look at it in detail.

"This is incredible, Sara. Thank you."

She preened at the praise. It was one thing to admire something you created but quite another to have someone else admire it.

"Can I collect it tomorrow?"

"Yes. It'll be ready for transport this time tomorrow."

"Perfect. Thank you again for your hard work."

"I'm happy to have been given the opportunity."

Xander looked at the painting again and felt his breath taken away once more. The landscape had more depth and beauty than a photograph of the area. It somehow had heart and the details were incredible. The more he looked, the more he saw the tinier touches. It was somehow even better than he had hoped, and he knew that Mara would love it.

Having seen it, he decided that a simple, thin black frame would be best. He didn't want anything that would detract from the art itself. Xander left the room and went directly to his car so he could get to Charlottesville before the shops closed. He wanted everything to be perfect for his evening with Mara. It was the closest thing they'd had to a date in many years.

---

Mara refused to admit it, but she was nervous about her dinner with Xander. She told herself that they were simply friends catching up, but he had acted a little odd. He had done the same thing in the past before he did something special. She smoothed her hands over her dress and smiled. It wouldn't be such a bad thing if he did do something special. They had spent more time together since he had been poisoned and she found herself enjoying his company once more.

There was still the past between them. They had both hurt the other by hiding important things but were moving on. A soft knock sounded at the door and Mara headed down the stairs of her small cottage and let Xander in. She shook her head when she saw the large rectangular package in the man's arms. Whatever it was, he had wrapped it himself in white paper with pale blue flowers. She knew he had done the wrapping because the edges were uneven and there was an excess of tape.

"Come in. I'll open a bottle of wine."

Xander removed his shoes before he followed Mara into her cottage. He placed the gift carefully on the couch before he joined her in the kitchen where she opened a bottle of red wine.

She handed him a glass and he breathed in the rich redcurrant and oak aroma with a smile. She'd remembered his favorite wine. He took that as a positive sign for the evening.

"I brought you a little something."

Mara laughed. "It doesn't look all that little."

Xander turned and walked into the living room with a grin. He had seen a large space on her living room wall near the main bookshelf where the painting would look perfect. The frame he had chosen blended beautifully with the rest of her decor.

"Would you care to open it?"

She sat beside the gift and placed her wine on the small table at the end of the couch. Carefully, she opened it and did her best to preserve the paper. Once the painting was revealed, she allowed herself to drink in the details. It was stunning. The view was one of her favorites and the artist had captured it beautifully. Everything she loved about the scene was there—the way the sun filtered through the leaves in the late afternoon and how the mountains glistened as though polished.

"Xander, this is too much."

"No. You have been very good to me over the years. This is exactly right."

Mara smiled and gazed at the painting once again. She knew that she would find more details over the coming months and years. He couldn't have chosen a better gift.

CHAPTER TWENTY-FIVE

Raine had quietly looked forward to potions. She felt as though she had progressed with them, and Evie had helped her understand all the various cooking terms. They'd spent Sunday afternoon in the kitchen with Tori and the other pixies, laughing and learning. Raine had a fantastic time and now walked into the potion's lab with a smile on her face. She felt ready to face whatever potion Professor Fowler had waiting for them.

Evie sat with Sara, so she could help remind her of the cooking terms. The kitsune had greatly improved on that front but still struggled a little. Raine sat with Adrien and William with Philip. The elf sighed when he saw the recipe sheet on their desk. Raine frowned when she read it through. It was far more complicated than anything they'd done before.

"Today, you will begin with a sleep potion. Then you will move onto a paralysis potion and its antidote." The professor put her hands behind her back. "I suggest you begin immediately and pay very close attention to the recipes."

"I'll help you with the spell parts." Adrien pointed to the recipe. "Don't worry, I'm sure it's far easier than it looks."

Raine read the recipe once more and saw that they needed to cast a spell on the honey to realign its essence and open it to the magic in the potion itself. Then, there were four stages to the actual potion. She wasn't entirely sure how they would fit three potions into the time allotted but she was always ready for a challenge.

Adrien spooned the honey into the small white ceramic dish, mouthed the words of the spell, and felt his magic rise as he did so. He went over the words with Raine to make sure her pronunciation was correct before they wove the spell together. She felt his cool magic against her warm one and watched as the honey bubbled beneath their combined enchantments. Things were going well so far.

Sara lost the confidence she'd felt when she walked into the room when she saw the complex spell. She had expected something far simpler like they had worked on previously. That was something she could do. Evie squeezed her hand and reminded her that she was right there and they'd do it together. They began by weaving the magic around the lavender and moved on to the spell over the honey.

She felt her kitsune magic stir within her. Something was happening, and she was glad of it. When the time came, she would be ready to embrace that side of her power. For now, she whispered the words over the honey and watched with delight as it bubbled perfectly.

Raine stirred the warm milk in a steady figure-of-eight

motion while Adrien pasted the honey and lavender mix onto the thin strip of tissue-thin white paper. He fed the paper slowly into the milk as Raine continued to stir while she whispered the next spell under her breath. The recipe had been very specific that the words must be whispered to aid in restfulness and quiet.

The elf took over the stirring and she added three drops of vanilla essence, which the recipe said was for extra sweet dreams. They watched the cauldron very closely as the creamy mixture began to simmer. The moment it had simmered for exactly ten seconds, Adrien removed it from the heat and stirred it counter-clockwise. The potion turned a delicate gray color, exactly as described in the recipe. They'd done it.

A sense of accomplishment filled Raine and she planned to tell Librarian Decker when she visited the library later. She knew he'd be proud of her too.

To Professor Fowler's surprise and pleasure, everyone had succeeded and brewed the sleeping potion perfectly. She normally had some problems with that one due to the number of smaller spells involved.

"Now, you will move on to the paralysis spell. I must remind you that any student found using this on another student will be punished."

Raine was excited to master this potion. It was something else that would be very useful to her as an agent.

"Are there any risks with this spell?" She raised her hand after she'd asked the question. "I mean, if we were to use it on someone, what are the potential problems and side-effects?"

"Well, too large a dose would lead to long-term paralysis and potentially death."

"Thank you." She read through the recipe that appeared on her desk.

The paralysis potion wasn't as complex as the sleep potion, but it required far more precision.

"Please note that if you do not brew this potion correctly there are risks of boils, blindness, and potentially, limbs falling off."

Sara gasped. "For us or the person who drinks it?"

The professor smiled. "The person who drinks it, although please do remember to wear your gloves at all times when you brew or handle this potion."

Raine pulled on her thick rubber gloves and picked up the pufferfish skin. She dropped that into the bottom of the cauldron along with Adrien's magpie feather and Komodo dragon tooth. They added a cup of water and three drops of spider venom and stirred slowly eight times as they watched the potion change to a deep bruise-purple. Once that color was achieved, they let it sit for six minutes and ten seconds.

During that time, Raine ground the vampire bat fangs with the belladonna, dragon snap, and forget-me-not. She had to really put her weight into it and work to grind it down into the required coarse texture before the timer went off. Adrien wrote the delicate runes on the black paper with the blood-red pen and dropped that into the absolute center of the potion. After exactly ninety-two seconds, Raine poured her powder into the potion.

They watched it for another three minutes before Adrien stirred it. The potion began to turn a violent green before ripples of electric blue spread outwards from the center. She was confident they had it right. They were careful, and the colors matched what was described on the recipe.

William breathed a sigh of relief when he saw the paralysis potion color shift slowly into a deep plum-purple. He watched it very closely and worried for a moment when the ripples looked closer to turquoise than what he thought of as electric blue. The potion emitted one small bubble and the half-Ifrit allowed himself to smile. They'd done it.

# CHAPTER TWENTY-SIX

Philip had spoken with the headmistress and Professor Fowler. The Entrepreneurs Club made focus potions to help the juniors and seniors with their big projects and the exams that were scheduled in a couple of months. It meant that Philip now frowned at a large cauldron full of bubbling blue liquid. He double-checked the recipe and was reassured that the potion was, in fact, the right color.

Professor Fowler had agreed to give the entire group extra credit for making the potions, and the money made from selling them went into their college funds. Philip stirred the mixture carefully in a slow, methodical fashion while he thought about the best way to market them. He knew that word of mouth would soon get around, but they needed to get the word out to begin with. Posters felt amateurish. He wanted something a little more business-like.

The wizard was lost in thought about how best to handle supply and demand when the timer dinged and he realized the potion was done. He removed the large cauldron from the heat and ladled the potion into small, delicate vials. Angeline had hand-written all the labels and it was his task to add the potion to the vials.

"We've been given space to store them." James looked up from his notes. "And Bella is working on the lock spells to make sure no one tries to help themselves."

Everything was coming together. They'd been careful to make sure the potion had no side-effects and no chances of addiction. Once the exam season was over, they would no longer sell it. It was a seasonal thing they'd pick up again the next spring.

---

Evie took great pleasure in beating the butter block into submission to make the dough for croissant and pain au choc. The butter was cool and needed a good deal of elbow grease to flatten into the main dough. Tori had magic she used when she made the pastries, but Evie liked the satisfaction that came with doing it by hand.

She hoped to finally perfect her croissant rolling today. Little by little, she had been getting closer, but they were such a delicate pastry that it took a long time to achieve the right consistency. Sara had joined her in the kitchen that day. Rose watched as the kitsune pressed thin pie pastry carefully into small casings to make tiny chocolate tarts. They'd be topped with gold foil when they were ready. Sara had worked hard to make sure everything was perfect and the pixies were pleased with her dedication.

Once Evie finished working the butter block into the

dough, she began the long process of folding, rolling, and re-folding the mixture until the layers were accomplished. She enjoyed the more physical work. There was something therapeutic about it. Nothing really got to her and everything washed off her like water off a duck's back.

Sara chewed on her bottom lip as she placed the baking beads into the pie casings. She wanted everything to be perfect. Evie produced such beautiful baked goods that she didn't want to let her friend down with something that wasn't up to scratch. Rose placed the pie casings in the oven and showed her what to look for. Sara had never thought she'd enjoy baking, but she slowly came around to the idea. There was a lot of fun to be had, and she could bring out her artistic side with the decorating.

***

Raine fastened her riding hat and smiled at the bright sunny day. Smoke had shown no concern over having a saddle buckled tight, so it was time to add weight to his back. Horace led the horse out into the middle of the arena and she moved a mounting block slowly beside him. The groundskeeper gave the young horse enough lead rope to look around and sniff at the mounting block. Once he was satisfied it wouldn't bite him, she stepped onto it and ran her hands over his back and ribs.

The horse snorted and shook his head a little before he shifted his weight to rest one of his back feet. Raine, satisfied that he was completely relaxed, leaned over his back. Smoke's ears flicked, but he remained entirely unconcerned. Cautiously, she leaned farther and finally rested her full weight on his back with her upper half hanging over his far side.

He looked at her and sniffed before he sighed in boredom.

"Are you ready?" Horace asked.

"Yep."

He encouraged Smoke to step forward slowly. Raine braced herself before she relaxed entirely and allowed her body to mold over his. Smoke walked a full lap around the arena without a care in the world. Raine slid off and grinned before she patted his neck and gave him a mint. She hoped today's success meant he'd be a breeze under saddle. Horace handed her the lead rope and she led him to the side where she put his surcingle on and proceeded to long-rein him and put him through lateral work. After ten minutes, she moved onto the school grounds as she wanted to accustom him to walking into strange places without her leading him. He walked with confidence and curiosity.

Raine felt sure that he would make a fantastic eventing horse. The only thing he ever batted an eye at was rain, but he could work through that. And if she was honest, no one really liked to stand out in the rain.

# CHAPTER TWENTY-SEVEN

Raine helped Evie pack the food into her backpack while Philip double-checked that they had enough to drink. Cameron carried the blanket and constantly shifted his weight. They had checked that they had everything for the past fifteen minutes and he was ready to head out into the beautiful day.

When Evie and Philip were both satisfied, they picked up the backpacks and set off for a day of relaxation. The clear blue sky stretched overhead without a single fluff of white in view. Students sat on the well-kept grass and laughed and joked. Raine saw two girls reading and almost envied them. Cameron entwined his fingers with hers and that envy slipped away. They had decided to make the most of the spring weather and head to the river for a picnic.

Evie had made the bread fresh for the sandwiches with the help of the pixies. Sara and Raine had helped make the small tartelettes for dessert, and the guys had found the drinks and candies. Cameron ran his thumb over Raine's and she felt a warmth fill her, a happiness that she hadn't felt before. The group walked in a comfortable silence across the gently rolling grass. The horses could be seen enjoying their paddocks in the distance. Raine had led Smoke out to his which he shared with Cloud and Murphy. The young horse had raced around the space and bucked exuberantly, clearly enjoying the sun on his back.

"I think this is the first day in months that we haven't needed to worry about homework." Evie wound her arm around William's. "It feels weird."

"You're worrying that we've forgotten something." He looked at her. "We went through everything. We have this day completely free to relax."

"We've earned this." Sara spun with her arms outstretched. "We've been cooped up forever. It feels good to have the sun on my skin and let go for a while."

Philip put his hands in his pockets and made a mental note to look for a potion or spell that allowed you to capture the feeling of the sun on your skin. That was something with many uses from helping people with SAD to adding something special to a party. He was sure there had to be something in the library.

Cameron found that everything was a little brighter and easier when he was around Raine. His wolf side quieted and the slight tightness that came from being in his human form for extended periods eased. He still wanted to feel her fingers running through his fur and hoped that they'd maybe have a chance for some quiet alone time soon. They'd all been so busy with their schoolwork there hadn't been much opportunity for anything like that.

They stepped into the cool shade of the woods and took a moment to allow their eyes to adjust to the change in light. The speckles of sunlight stretched between the shadows and made Sara itch to paint. She had given serious consideration to taking up photography exactly for moments like that. While she adored painting, it was also time-consuming and photography had a very different feel to it. She took her time and absorbed the way the sunlight caught the angles and dips in the bark on the mature trees and the leaves almost seemed to glow. Yes, photography was something she would seriously look into. Her birthday was in the summer. Perhaps her family would come together to get her a camera.

Raine led the way down the shallow bank toward the perfect spot for their picnic—a stretch of open grass near the riverbank. The sunlight warmed the earth beneath them and they set up the picnic. The navy-blue blanket was stretched out to give everyone room to sit comfortably. Food and drink were placed in the middle, so everyone could easily reach it, and paper plates and cups were passed around. Cameron sat near Raine with his legs stretched out beside hers.

"This food looks incredible." Adrien placed a sandwich onto his plate. "I don't know how I'll survive as a poor student when I can't afford this sort of food."

Everyone laughed.

"You'll live on ramen and pop tarts." Sara grinned and took a sandwich for herself. "That's the usual student diet, isn't it?"

"I don't think I've ever had ramen." Adrien frowned

before he bit into his sandwich. "I think I'll have to learn how to bake. This bread is perfection."

Evie blushed, and William squeezed her hand.

"Have you heard that new band everyone's talking about?" The half-Ifrit looked around the group. "I haven't managed to get my hands on their music yet."

"Riot of the Storms? The indie rock one?" Cameron handed Raine a little chocolate tartelette. "I've heard people talk about them but I haven't tried to find the music."

"Oh, I have them on my phone." Philip pulled out his phone and found the music. "I downloaded their first album this morning." He pressed play.

Raine wasn't keen on the first song. It wasn't to her taste with an almost sharp metallic undertone that set her teeth on edge. She much preferred more traditional rock and the eighties stuff her uncle loved listening to.

"Not my thing." Sara shrugged and picked up a mini apple pie. "These desserts, however, are to die for."

"This is definitely the best picnic I've ever had." Cameron stretched and poured himself a cup of ginger ale. "We need more afternoons like this."

Heavy footsteps approached the group from the woodland. Cameron's ears pricked, and he turned to see who came toward them. Raine followed his gaze but the others ignored it, assuming it was an older student or teacher checking up on them. Adrien felt something shift around him, a tickle of familiar magic. He turned to see the man who had approached him in the kemana step out of the woods. He had a friend with him this time.

The smaller blond man sneered at Adrien. "So that's the little elf."

Adrien rolled his eyes and stood. Cameron and Raine did as well. She had her wand drawn in case she needed to defend her friends.

"Oh, don't be so melodramatic." The dark-eyed man rolled his eyes. "We're simply here to talk."

He took a step closer to the group who all stood their ground.

"How did you get onto the school grounds?" Adrien glared at them. "There are wards."

The man shrugged. "We're not here to cause you any harm, so we slipped through. We have our ways."

Raine quietly decided to speak to Agent Connor once this was over to see if those wards could be updated. That seemed like a security risk.

"We're only here to talk." The blond smiled and showed too many teeth. "Adrien, you really should listen."

"Your family is not what you have been told. They slaughtered a great many people only last year. Do you know how much blood is on their hands?" The dark man put his hands in his pockets as if to make himself less threatening. "Would protectors really kill people?"

"Yes." Raine stared the man down. "Sometimes it's better for the world if bad people lose their lives. They can no longer cause harm and damage."

"And who exactly decides who those bad people are?" The man pursed his lips. "You?"

She folded her arms, careful to keep a good grip on her wand.

"That's what laws were made for." She lifted her chin. "When people break the law, they suffer the consequences."

"And what if people who made those laws are wrong?" The blond man shifted his weight. "What then?"

Raine rolled her eyes.

"The laws are made through a democracy. They're made for the greater good of society." She sighed, weary of this conversation. "The government is in the best position to decide which laws are necessary. That is why they exist."

"Come and speak to us privately, Adrien." The dark-haired man opened his arms to the elf. "Let us show you what you have been missing."

"I don't think that'll be necessary." He folded his arms and refused to budge. "I am well aware of my family's long history and position in the world."

The blond man moved to walk toward the elf, but his companion used his arm to stop him.

"Until next time."

The men turned and walked away through the woods.

"What was that all about?" Sara looked at Adrien. "Is everything okay?"

"Fine. My family is strong and holds a position of power amongst the guardians and protectors in France." He sat again. "Some of the less respected families try to interfere sometimes. It's all talk, nothing to worry about."

"It's so cool that you're a guardian like that." Sara grinned at him. "And your family's done that for generations?"

"Yes. We work closely with the police and others to ensure the safety of the humans around us. We also maintain balance within the magical community."

"I think I should tell Agent Connor about this." Raine looked at the woods. "He should know that potentially dangerous men wandered onto the school grounds to harass a student."

Sara looked longingly at the Reese's peanut butter cups they had been saving. The picnic had been going so beautifully until those men showed up.

# CHAPTER TWENTY-EIGHT

Raine knocked on Agent Connor's office door and waited patiently. They had packed up the picnic and returned to the school. The mood had been spoiled by the intrusion of the men trying to talk to Adrien.

The agent wasn't normally in his office on the weekend but Raine had spotted his little sign showing he was around. Her only other option was to go to his cottage, but the teachers' cottages were strictly off limits for the students. Footsteps approached the door and the agent opened it. He greeted Raine with a surprised smile and gestured for her to step inside.

"Would you like to speak to your uncle?"

He put his hands in the pockets of his dark slacks and smiled at her.

"Oh, no. Thank you. I'm actually here to discuss an incident with you." She took a deep breath. "We were having a picnic down by the river when a pair of older men—in their late thirties, I believe—approached us. They wanted to speak to my friend Adrien specifically. He's the French elf from a family of guardians and protectors. They wanted to speak to him about his family and proceeded to try to convince him that his family were bad people. I believe their purpose was to bring him around to their way of thinking and draw him into their fold. Adrien wasn't interested, and the men left. My concern is that they were able to get onto the grounds and knew where to find us."

The agent pursed his lips and handed Raine a notebook and pen. "If you could write down a full description of the men, that would be useful."

She jotted down everything she could think of, from the well-worn jeans to the small holes in the corners of the dark-haired one's jacket. When done, she handed the notebook back to the agent who smiled at her detail.

"Thank you, Raine. I'll speak to the headmistress. You don't need to worry. This won't happen again."

Raine nodded politely and left the office. Bruce looked at the notes and added his own about the location and history of Adrien's family. He left his office and walked to the headmistress'. The wards and protections needed to be updated to take this new information into account, but he couldn't do that himself.

He knocked on the door and smiled as he heard Xander's voice in the office with Mara. The voices stopped, and she opened the door.

"Is everything okay, Bruce?"

The agent looked up and down the hallway for students who might overhear. "I believe we should tweak the security around the grounds to be safe."

Mara stepped aside and encouraged him to enter her office. "What happened?"

"Raine came to me and said a pair of men approached her friend Adrien. She gave me this description." He handed her the notebook. "They didn't attempt violence, but the risk is present enough that I believe it would be a good idea to tighten security."

Xander frowned and glanced at the notebook. "I will speak to the pixies and the others. We have avoided taking such extreme measures as it can be difficult to change the wards to allow parents and expected visitors onto the grounds. There are methods that can be used, however. Thank you, Bruce." The professor smiled. "We appreciate your help and diligence in keeping the school safe."

"Not to worry. I'll look down in the woods for any trace of them." He turned toward the door. "Thanks for taking this seriously."

"Of course. The safety of the students is our top priority." Mara smiled. "We'll call on the others now."

Once Bruce had left the office Mara sighed and Xander leaned back on her desk.

"We'll have to use heavier wards and give expected visitors runes to allow them through." The professor dragged his fingers through his hair. "It'll be a logistical nightmare, and even then, determined people will still be able to replicate the runes."

The headmistress pursed her lips. "I don't believe there's a way to truly keep people off the grounds, not without making it permanent. That starts to feel too much like a prison, though. We will gather the others to strengthen the wards and make them more discerning about who is allowed on the grounds."

Xander nodded and smiled weakly. "Will you still join me for dinner once we're done?"

"I wouldn't miss it." She laid her hand on his. "I've enjoyed our dinners together."

# CHAPTER TWENTY-NINE

Raine pulled her blankets up tighter around her. The room seemed very cold and she peered into the darkness, her eyes still bleary from sleep.

"Did someone break the heating?" Sara groaned and pulled a hoodie over her pajamas. "I'm sure I have frostbite."

"I have no idea." Raine fumbled for her thick fluffy socks. "I thought the heating was magical."

"It is." Christie hid her head under her blankets.

"We should investigate." Raine pulled her socks on and dragged her jeans on over her pajamas. "People could be suffering."

"I know I am." Sara wrapped a second scarf around her neck. "Kitsunes aren't great in the cold."

Evie had bundled up in everything she had close to hand. Christie remained hidden beneath her mountain of blankets. Raine led the small group to the door which she opened and then stopped dead.

The hallway had a dense carpet of snow and more fell from the ceiling. Laughter echoed around them. Raine stepped into the snowy hallway and saw a fellow freshman witch slide down the stairs on the thick layer of snow. Banks piled up at the edges of the corridor and the snow seemed to fall even more heavily on the floor below them.

"It's April Fools." Evie massaged her temples. "This must be a prank."

"It's pretty cool, actually." Sara looked around them. "No pun intended."

The girls slid down the compacted snow covering the staircase. Cameron bounded toward them in his large wolf form. He grinned and bent into a playful bow in front of Raine. She laughed and ran after him when he spun and raced off down the hallway. As other students woke, more laughter filled the school.

The entire building had been turned into a snowy wonderland. A snowman competition began in the dining hall and Raine couldn't resist joining in. She and Evie gathered snow to make the base. Cameron remained in his wolf form and nosed snow toward them. He leaned on the ball and added pawprints where the buttons would traditionally be. Their snowman was in the classic shape complete with borrowed hat and scarf. Raine was reminded of fun-filled winters with her uncle and friends.

Mara sighed as she looked at the mayhem all around her. She wasn't sure which student had done it, but the magic was complicated, and the students were having a ball. Once she'd found the threads of the spell, she decided to give everyone one more hour of enjoyment before she returned the school to its usual state. Someone had made a life-size dragon out of snow in the dining hall. Given the detail of the scales and wings, she suspected it was the pixies. She couldn't blame them—a large part of her wanted to join in and make snow sculptures too.

A snowball hit her back. She turned with her fiercest glare only to see Xander grinning at her like a fool with snow in his hair. Mara laughed and formed her own snowball to throw back at him. As April Fools pranks went, she felt this was one of the better ones. The spell would leave no destruction in its wake, and it was fun.

# CHAPTER THIRTY

Philip put the DVD in the player and hit play. Adrien grinned as he opened his bag of freshly popped popcorn with extra cheese.

"Thanks, guys. I'm not really a party person. Watching *Salem's Lot* with my friends is my idea of a perfect birthday celebration." The elf put some popcorn in his mouth. "I know it doesn't entirely fall into old cheesy horror, but hopefully, it's close enough that you'll all enjoy it."

Philip poured everyone a glass of sparkling grape juice and passed the glasses around to everyone while the opening scene played.

"To Adrien. May he have many more happy birthdays." Philip raised his glass. "To many more years of happiness and success."

Everyone clinked their glass and wished him a happy birthday before they settled. Cameron put his arm around Raine's shoulders and she leaned into him. Sara added extra M&Ms into her popcorn and everyone watched the first real scene in fascination.

"I like those old jeeps." William nodded at the jeep on screen. "I wouldn't have one in cream, though."

"In a nice high-shine black." The shifter offered Raine some of his beef jerky. "It'd look badass with some big all-terrain tires too."

"They really like the creepy dramatic music in the opening to these older horrors," Evie commented before she bit into her Twizzler. "Do they do that in modern ones?"

"I think so," Raine affirmed. "I haven't watched many."

"Oh, he's suspicious." Sara pointed to the tv. "A guy comes into a small town with no family. He's either the vampire or the hunter. I'll bet on vampire since he's interested in the house on the hill."

"I do love the over the top house on the hill aesthetic." Raine moved her blanket to cover both her and Cameron's laps. "You know the gothic dark ones with the huge, creepy iron gates, gargoyles, and all that?"

"Yes." Cameron grinned. "I wouldn't live in one, but I don't think I'd be able to resist exploring one. I know they're a classic and it'd be full of vampires and mad scientists, but I'd have to check it out."

William laughed. "You'd never make it through a horror movie. Although I don't think I would either. I'm sure I'd make the same silly decisions they do."

Evie laughed and scooted a little closer to him.

"Raine would survive a horror movie." Adrien smiled at her. "She's far too pragmatic to fall for all those tricks."

"That depends," she responded thoughtfully. "If I heard

a scream from inside that creepy house or a cry for help, I'd run right in there. I'd definitely go and find you guys if you vanished somewhere."

"We'd all be doomed." Philip laughed. "At least we'd be doomed together, right?"

"Definitely." Adrien refilled his grape juice. "I can't imagine a better group of people to be caught in a horror movie with."

"We should take bets on who's the vampire and who's the hunter." Sara gestured with a piece of popcorn between her fingers. "Is that the plotline of this movie? I haven't read the book and I assumed it was."

"Kind of." Adrien made a back and forth motion with his hand. "He's not Van Helsing, but there is a guy who kills vampires."

"Okay." Sara looked triumphant. "So, I think that writer guy is the vampire. There's something suspicious about him."

"No, my money's on the guy in the house on the hill being the vampire," Cameron said firmly. "There's something about the creepy house on the hill—it's a classic after all."

"I'm saying nothing." Adrien put his hands up. "I've read the book."

"I have to agree with Cameron," Raine said firmly. "I think the house on the hill guy is the vampire. It's such a popular idea."

"I really want to fix his crooked collar." Evie pointed at the man on the tv. "One side sticks out over his jacket and I'm itching to fix it."

William smiled at her. He liked those things about Evie,

like the way small creases formed around her eyes when something small bugged her far more than she felt it should.

"Are they snooping around the writer's room?" Sara put another M&M in her mouth. "That's so rude. I'd be livid if someone did that to me."

"That's why you use spells to ward your room and stop snoops," the elf pointed out. "Nothing to hurt them, simply something to make sure they know you know."

"That jeep wasn't moving." William pointed at the tv. "There's no engine noise and the movement was weird."

"Can you imagine acting that?" Adrien frowned. "Pretending you're in a moving car and trying to ignore all the cameras and things."

"I couldn't be an actor," Raine decided. "I don't have it in me. I'm me. I can't put on a facade or play a part."

"That's part of what I like about you," Cameron said and squeezed her arm. "You're so entirely you."

"I have two questions." Sara lifted two fingers. "One. If vampires can't see their reflections, how do they dress so well? Two, relating to that, why do they always dress so smartly? They're always in custom suits and things."

"Well, if the suits are made to order, you know they fit well." Philip shrugged. "So that clears up the reflection part."

"And I think it's because vampires have lots of money," Adrien ventured. "They wear suits to reflect that."

"But that doesn't make much sense. Not everyone is good with money, and surely they don't only turn rich people?" Sara sighed. "They could make a mistake and lose lots of money. Surely people who dress like those around them blend in better too. A guy in a hoodie with jeans and work boots wouldn't turn as many heads or be as memorable as someone in a very nice suit."

"That depends on the setting," Raine interjected. "If they work in the high-end part of London or New York or somewhere similar, tailored suits would be the norm."

Sara wrinkled her nose.

"I agree with you." William nudged Sara gently. "I think it's a bit weird."

"The patterns on the clothes were much louder back then," Philip commented. "You wouldn't see someone walking to work with such a bold pattern on their shirt these days."

"There's something to be said for bold patterns." Sara smoothed out her skirt. "Sometimes, they can look amazing. It's about making sure they work for you."

"Ah, look. The man on the hill's from Europe," Evie said. "That's a sure sign that he's the vampire. I bet he's even from Transylvania or at least Romania."

"Oh, that man in the hat gets my vote for the hunter," Cameron added. "Look at the expression on his face."

"How would you defend yourself from vampires?" Philip looked at the others. "Garlic and a cross? A stake to the heart? Which would you think are real?"

"Stake to the heart and decapitation." Raine nodded firmly. "Nothing can survive decapitation."

"Garlic never made any sense to me. Does anyone know where that one came from?" Evie looked at Adrien. "Any ideas?"

"I know this one." William grinned. "They believe it came from an unusual disease called porphyria which causes sensitivity to sunlight, a drawn appearance, and problems with sulfur-rich foods such as garlic."

"Oh, that's actually tragic," Sara muttered. "Those poor people suffered from a horrible disease that likely hurt, and the people around them thought they were monsters."

"That's human nature." Cameron rubbed his thumb over Raine's shoulder. "Fear is a powerful thing, and people are terrified of what they don't understand."

"That's why we're helping people understand magic." Raine leaned into the shifter. "And it's why the government works hard to unify the humans and the magicals because we can do so much when we work together."

"Sorry to change the topic, but I didn't see this becoming one where everyone turns into a vampire," Sara said as she finished the last of her popcorn. "I expected it to be a classic vampire versus hunter tale."

"Well, this is by Steven King and he does have his own brand of horror." Adrien smiled. "Have you seen any movie adaptations of his others?"

"I saw the fog? The mist?" William frowned as he tried to remember. "The ending of that! I think it was very King and very memorable."

"He does enjoy looking at people and the way they come together and fall apart," Philip concurred. "I haven't read much by him, but I know his reputation."

"So… Why didn't the guy fight back? And perhaps more importantly, why on Earth was there a set of antlers? Not one pair, but what was that? A dozen antlers on the wall like that?" Philip folded his arms. "The man should at least have kicked."

Raine had watched the scene where the vampire picked

a man up by the upper arms and walked him calmly to the antlers where he impaled him. She'd asked herself the same questions. The man's legs were free, he could have kicked, and his hands were free to claw at the vampire's eyes. The antlers seemed to be there purely for impaling people, which seemed an odd choice. But she wasn't a vampire, so maybe it made more sense to them.

Sara shook her head as she saw the guy change his mind on which ankle he had supposedly twisted.

"You know, when they first said he was into collecting antiques, I'd expected his house to be full of beautiful old European furniture." William leaned a little closer to Evie. "I have yet to see one nice antique. The house is full of stuffed pelicans, antelopes, and way too many antlers."

"He definitely does not live up to the idea of the beautiful mansion with expensive old everything," Cameron agreed. "I suppose he's a little closer to the old myths—needing to be near the dirt and all. If I was a vampire, I'd have to be the type that had the nice mansion and wore fancy suits. I couldn't give up being a shifter, though. I'd have to be old school and maintain my ability to shift into a wolf."

"I like that plan." Evie smiled at him. "You'd have the best of all worlds that way."

"Why do vampires sleep in coffins?" Sara asked the others. "It'd freak me out. I'd want a nice comfortable bed."

"Well, a coffin is entirely impenetrable to sunlight, and no normal person would open a closed casket." William shrugged. "That's my theory, anyway."

"There's another theory that they sleep the sleep of the dead, so returning to a coffin is something that ties into that." Evie wrinkled her nose. "I don't like that theory as much though."

"I know back in the old days when there was a vampire scare, they'd dig up the old bodies—" William stopped himself and frowned. "I started that in the wrong place. So, back then, people would become unconscious and maybe even go into a kind of coma, often thanks to ergot poisoning. They'd be buried because people thought they were dead. When there was a vampire scare, the people would dig the bodies up and find the now dead people twisted and covered in blood from when they tried to escape and died horribly. They therefore thought the vampires slept in their coffins during the day."

"That really is horrifying." Sara wrapped her blanket more tightly around her. "The past sounds awful."

"Oh, there are all sorts of awful things like that," Evie added. "There was a time when they put a string into the coffin with a bell attached. If the person wasn't dead, they'd ring the bell and be dug up again. Or so they hoped."

"Her dress is really pretty." Sara pointed at the woman in the coffin on the screen. "Although it looks like she's a bride of the vampire. I don't like that. If I let a vampire turn me, I'd want my freedom. None of this bride stuff."

"I do find the bond between sire and new vampire interesting," Philip commented thoughtfully. "I wonder what forms that. Is it the sharing of magic between them that allows the new vampire to become a vampire?"

"I wouldn't sign up for the sire being able to control me, though." Cameron frowned. "It's one thing to have an alpha you respect, but someone who can actually control you thanks to this bond? And you're stuck with them for hundreds of years?"

"It'd really suck if the myth where you kill the sire and all the vampires they had made die was true." William shifted his weight. "One minute, you're walking along minding your own business, and the next, you're ash because your sire whom you haven't seen in three hundred years received a stake to the heart."

Everyone laughed.

"Well, the ending to that movie wasn't quite what I expected." Sara shrugged. "It was fun, though."

"Did you enjoy it, Adrien?" Raine looked to the elf. "Anything else we can do to make your birthday special?"

"I'm looking forward to my cake after dinner." He grinned and stood. "I know Evie's baking is truly exceptional."

Evie blushed.

"I hope you like it."

"I'm sure I'll love it."

# CHAPTER THIRTY-ONE

This was it. Adrien jogged on the spot to loosen his muscles. They were playing the game that would win or lose them the championship and this was the culmination of a year's work. The team had trained exceptionally hard. Cody and Daniel had perfected new tracking spells and they had all spent many hours going over the assault course and honing their magic.

Matt rolled his shoulders. He had a good feeling about this match. The team was strong and cohesive.

They walked onto the field to the cheering of the crowds. The stands were packed with spectators. Adrien didn't think he'd seen that many people in one space before. They'd all come to see them win the championship and the pressure was daunting.

The team stood in the middle of the field and waited. Etienne squeezed his brother's shoulder, a small mark of solidarity. They had always gotten along well.

To Adrien's horror, the field gave way to a wide ocean.

He began swimming almost immediately, but he didn't appreciate having his clothes soaked. The gentle swells glittered like diamonds under the burning sun. Matt led the group toward a desert island with a thick covering of palm trees. It looked idyllic like something ripped from an old travel brochure or a movie. Adrien was sure that meant it was rampant with traps and enemies.

They pulled themselves from the water and jogged across the soft white beach sand. Matt turned slowly and surveyed their surroundings while the elves drew their swords. Cody and Daniel raised their wands, alert for any sign of danger.

The only sound was the gentle lap of waves on the beach. It was too perfect. Matt was about to lead them into the dark forest when the ground began to shake. Sand whipped up and formed a clear line which headed straight for them. They had no idea what it was but they ran into the forest as quickly as they could.

Raine gasped when a large black worm erupted from the sand and clamped its beak-like mouth onto thin air where Adrien had been only a second before. The elf ran deeper into the forest and hacked through the thick vines and branches as he went. It wasn't the best use for his sword, but it worked.

Once they were safely away from the beach, they slowed their pace and looked around them for clues about where they should be heading. Matt pricked his ears and sniffed the wind. The silence ate at him. It was never a good sign in a landscape like that. It usually meant that bad things were lurking.

Cody spotted a rune carved into the trunk of one of the

trees ahead of them. Matt scrambled over the tall, exposed roots for a closer look. Etienne followed him, and Adrien stood guard, his senses trained for potential enemies. There was no way they would be allowed to continue through that jungle without further obstacles.

Daniel shouted when his feet were suddenly sucked downward into what had originally been solid ground. Adrien and Cody kneeled near him and worked rapidly through the spell that Professor Powell had taught them to counteract quicksand. Daniel slowed his breathing and calmed himself as much as possible. He knew that the more he struggled, the deeper he would be pulled down. The moment the soil was up to his stomach, he would vanish back to the field.

Cody and Adrien broke the spell and Daniel was spat back onto solid ground. He laid his palms flat on it and took a deep gulp of air. He hated quicksand.

Matt and Etienne decided that the rune pointed them north. They gestured for the others to follow and moved as quickly through the thick forest as they could manage. The two elves hacked through the foliage and vines in an effort to clear a path. It regrew as soon as they passed, which meant they had no idea where they had been or what might be behind them.

Slowly, the landscape changed and the thick-trunked trees and the heavy, dark-green vines that dangled from their low-hanging branches changed. The trees were now spaced farther apart, and the branches swayed far over-head. The small shrubs had been replaced by tall flowers with dark-purple leaves almost as big as Adrien was. Their flowers were vase-shaped in a peculiar shade of pink. He kept as far away from them as he was able.

They paused in a small clearing and searched for another rune or sign of where to go. One of the flowers shrank in on itself before it spat a large glob of something neon-yellow at Matt. The shifter darted to the side and watched in horror as the expectorate dissolved a large chunk of the tree next to him. The other flowers began to shrink down, and the guys raced deeper into the woods.

Adrien was painfully aware of the time ticking by. Who knew where their rivals were? They didn't even know if they were headed in the right direction. At least they hadn't seen any more of the acid-spitting flowers, so there was that. He hacked his way through a particularly dense section and finally spotted another rune. Symbols had never been his strong point. He held back and let the others examine it while he stood guard.

"It means we continue this way." Matt pointed. "Straight ahead."

"It feels wrong." Etienne folded his arms. "It feels like a trap."

Adrien saw the vines stirring. "Guys, hurry up and decide!" He slashed a vine down. "The vines are coming to life."

Right on cue, the creepers dropped and lashed out at the team.

"We go straight ahead!" Matt shouted and yanked a vine off Cody's back. "Now!"

Daniel grew sick and tired of the aggressive plants. He was wet, his clothes stuck to his back, and he had sand in his pants. The wizard formed a large fireball and set the vines on fire. A high-pitched, keening scream filled the air as the creepers shriveled and burned. He nodded with satisfaction. Daniel one, vines nil.

The air grew hot and thick around them. Their clothes clung to their skin and the team grew increasingly frustrated as they trekked through the jungle. Matt wondered if he'd read the rune wrong and they now moved in the wrong direction. Etienne saw the glint of gold ahead of them. He also saw the telltale flash of color from the rival team.

Matt and the others hurtled through the trees. They leapt over fallen logs and dodged vines that tried to drag them into the trees. The other team now ran for all they were worth toward the gold token which rested on a stone pedestal. A quiet voice in the back of Adrien's mind told him it was a trap, but he was exhausted and ready for a long, hot shower.

Etienne jumped first. The stone around the plinth vanished to leave a deep, dark pit, but the elf grasped the edge of the plinth. He hauled himself up and snatched the golden token. The rival team skidded to a halt at the edge of the chasm.

None of that mattered. The jungle faded, and the team was safely back on the field where people rushed out of the stands to lift them onto their shoulders. The players were carried around the field while everyone chanted and cheered. They'd done it. They'd won the championship.

# CHAPTER THIRTY-TWO

Xander had decided to mix things up in class. He planned to teach the students how to break through illusions. When used by a skilled practitioner, these could impact the physical body, which could, of course, cause real problems if applied correctly. Mara hadn't allowed him to try to teach freshmen illusions of that level, so he began with how to break through them.

"Today, you will learn how to break through an illusion." He ignored the groan of boredom. "As those of you who have studied will be aware, some illusions can impact the physical body. They convince your mind that they are so real that they can actually cause injuries or death."

That caught the class's attention.

"This means that understanding how to pull an illusion apart is a valuable skill." He leaned back against his desk. "First, you must be able to identify an illusion."

The students sat up and really focused now. The threat of death or dismemberment usually encouraged that.

"A well-formed illusion will be indistinguishable from your physical surroundings to your normal vision. You will need to rely on your magic and other senses. It is very difficult to form sounds via illusion, for example. If a sound seems off and you're in a situation where someone might feel the need to use an illusion, look around you with your magic."

He had explained how to look with their magic in the previous class, but a few students still looked confused and unsure.

"To look with your magic, you must find a state of calm and stretch your power around you. It works a little like sonar in that it will ping off your surroundings and give you an image of other magic that might be present. If you were to stretch your magic out to this chair to my left, you'd find it feels glassy. That is because it's an illusion."

He watched as the students each adopted expressions of deep concentration as they reached out with their magic.

Raine stretched her enchantment around her and reached out for the chair. It took her more effort than she would have liked but she managed it. The chair did feel cool and weirdly smooth, as the professor has said it would. Satisfied that she could feel what she was meant to feel, she waited for him to continue.

"Now, every illusion has edges. To undo an illusion, you must find those edges and pull them apart."

Raine once again stretched her power out and ran her magical fingers over the chair in search of edges. She found something slightly rough and ragged, tugged on it, and saw the chair shimmer and waver.

"Good! Now I will give you each a small illusion and you will pull it apart."

An ink pot and quill appeared out of thin air in front of Raine.

She scooted her chair back a little to see the entire illusion better and achieve a comfortable angle with her wand. Carefully, she examined it and it looked entirely physical. If she hadn't seen them appear, she would have assumed they were real. Raine reached out and found that her hand refused to get close enough to touch them.

"As Miss Campbell is demonstrating, many illusions of this style have a caveat in their casting that means your body won't allow you to touch them. Please note that these are different from those that would harm you. They can't, after all, harm you if they don't touch you."

Everyone turned to look at Raine who continued to try to touch the ink pot to demonstrate what the professor had said. The rest of the class proceeded to try to pick up their quill or ink pot and each of them failed.

Raine ceased her demonstration and pushed her magic into her wand to feel for the edges of the illusion. Once again, it felt cool and glassy beneath her magical senses. She pursed her lips as she focused on her task. After a few minutes, she still hadn't found them and grew frustrated.

"Remember to look with your magic, not your eyes." The professor walked between the desks. "Your eyes betray you."

Raine closed her eyes and tried again. It was a trust exercise because she didn't close her eyes around anyone but her friends and family. She had never understood how people could walk around with noise-canceling headphones.

Once more, she pushed her magic around the ink pot and quill in search of the edges of the illusion. It felt like it took an eternity, but she finally felt the first ragged thread. She tugged on it and the entire illusion quivered beneath her enchantment. The next edge came more easily, and she yanked on the thread there. The illusion began to collapse beneath her power. When she opened her eyes, she saw it flicker like a candle in the wind. That was enough to allow her to find the final thread.

She pulled the illusion apart and her desk now stood empty.

Sara glared at her ink pot. She had found the first edge but her embarrassment at being slower than the others clouded her ability to find the next. The more she felt others pull their illusions apart, the more her magic buckled and blocked her view. Philip put his hand on her arm and offered some support.

She calmed herself and regained control over her magic. Finally, she managed to find the next thread and yanked the illusion apart with a viciousness that reflected her humiliation. No one had watched her, not really, but it still hurt her to struggle. She took a calming breath and reminded herself that she was progressing. Her kitsune magic was waking.

# CHAPTER THIRTY-THREE

E vie had promised to teach her two friends how to make amazing cupcakes for any occasion. Raine was a little nervous as she hadn't done much baking. Cupcakes seemed simple, though, and Evie reassured them that they could apply hundreds of flavors to the simple cake mixture.

They walked into the kitchen to find Tori with a huge grin on her face.

"Oh, darlings! You can help me make scones. Don't worry, there'll be plenty of time to make your cupcakes too." The pixie handed them all aprons. "We'll show you how to add a little magic into your baking. You'll have everyone coming back for seconds and thirds."

Raine couldn't help but be swept up by Tori's bubbly enthusiasm. The cupcakes seemed far more doable with her helping them. The pixie guided them to Evie's work-station which had been expanded a little to make sure all three girls had plenty of room.

"These are both wonderfully easy recipes. You'll make them fancy in no time." Tori put the recipes down on the countertop. "Evie will look after you. I'll be back to help you put the magic into them."

Raine looked at the recipe and was relieved to find that it was, in fact, very simple. They mixed the ingredients and Evie explained how to be sure that it was light and fluffy enough.

"You want the butter and sugar to be really light and creamy. It should go a pale color." She put her spatula in and lifted some of the mixture. "Do you see how this is really airy? That will pass along into your cupcakes and make them feather-light."

Raine made notes in her notebook. She wanted to make sure she made them perfectly for her uncle over the summer holidays.

Evie encouraged her friends to make their own batches while she watched. Sara was cautious and overanalyzed everything. Baking had never been her forte, but she managed perfectly. Evie merely encouraged and reassured her.

Once the batter was complete, Tori came over and gathered the girls around her.

"Now, we add a little magic! We'll infuse a small dash of pleasure which will bring out the flavors." The pixie handed the girls a note with the words they should say. "On three."

Raine memorized the words, raised her wand, and pointed it at the batter. They all spoke the words together and pushed their magic into the mix.

Tori bustled away to make something else while the girls filled the cupcake wrappers. Evie put the trays into the oven and they all kept a close eye on them.

"You want them to be golden brown. They will get darker once you pull them out of the oven." Evie picked up a clean toothpick. "The best way to be sure they're done is to poke a toothpick in. If it comes out clean, they're done."

"Why a toothpick?" Sara frowned at it. "Why not a fork or something?"

"The batter won't stick to metal, whereas if it's uncooked, it will stick to wood."

Raine nodded, satisfied with that answer.

Evie pulled the batches of cupcakes out of the oven the moment they turned golden brown. She poked one with a toothpick but jumped back in horror when it squeaked.

"Are they meant to do that?" Sara looked from the cake to Evie. "I've never heard of a cupcake squeaking."

She approached to poke it once more.

The cake groaned. Tori came over to see what was going on. To everyone's horror, the cake spoke.

"I'm hot."

"Did that cupcake talk?" Sara backed away. "That definitely isn't normal."

"You're not normal," a different cupcake said.

The entire kitchen team gathered around and stared at the cupcakes. They looked perfectly normal, despite the fact that they had discovered speech.

Tori picked up a toothpick and went to poke at one.

"Ow. How would you feel if I poked you?"

The pixie's eyes went wide.

"You're not going to eat us, are you? You can't eat us."

Everyone looked at each other, feeling lost and horrified.

"I definitely can't eat something that talks to me." Raine shook her head. "That's a definite no."

"Has this ever happened before?" Evie looked at Tori. "Is this something you're familiar with?"

"No." Tori looked at Sara. "Wait, are you a kitsune?"

Sara looked at the floor. "Yeah."

Tori shook her head and laughed. "Don't worry, dear girl. It's my own fault. Kitsune magic reacts a little differently with some spells. It's the trickster nature of it." Tori looked at the cupcakes once more. "I'm not sure what we'll do with them, though."

"The headmistress can break the spell." A quiet pixie walked forward. "She's good with that stuff."

"Or that Professor Powell," another pixie said.

"You're going to kill us?"

"You're going to rip away our soul?"

"What did we do to deserve this?"

"We're innocent. We deserve to live!"

"You monsters!"

Tori shook her head.

"Well, this is one for the books." She looked at the quiet pixie. "Alex, would you mind fetching my spell book for me?"

Tori wouldn't lean on the headmistress. Her magic had helped do this, so she would undo it. The cupcakes began chanting that they deserved life.

Raine finally tired of this. "And what sort of life would you have? You will become old and stale and grow mold."

The cupcakes quieted before the center one spoke again.

"That is our decision to make."

"What if we want to grow mold?" another piped up.

"Exactly! Getting stale and moldy might feel good. That's our decision to make."

"I don't want to get mold."

"I want to see the world."

"You're a cupcake. Can you even see?" Evie put her hands on her hips. "How did we end up making the dramatic cupcakes?"

Everyone laughed.

"I might be able to see. You never know."

"How many fingers am I holding up?" Evie held three fingers over the cupcakes. "Hm?"

The cupcakes didn't respond.

"Who says the fingers really exist at all? This world could all be an illusion, nothing but a dream," one finally said.

"It feels surreal right now..." Sara rubbed her temples. "This is not how I thought this would go."

"Did a cupcake try to use weird philosophy to continue living and turn moldy?" Raine looked at the others. "Is that what happened?"

They all laughed again.

Alex returned with the spell book and one of the cupcakes emitted a banshee wail. Raine had very little patience with that and grabbed an icing bag.

"I'll cover you in frosting unless you stop that awful sound."

Silence reigned for a brief moment.

"What flavor frosting?"

"Lavender."

"I don't like lavender. I want chocolate."

"Lemon."

"Lemon sucks. Put vanilla on me."

"Vanilla is boring. Chocolate rules."

Raine sighed. At least they weren't wailing.

Tori flipped through her spell book and found something from her Aunt Nicole that dealt with exactly that situation. The pixie rolled her sleeves up and began to weave her magic.

"You can't do this!"

"We deserve life!"

She ignored them and worked through the spell that tore their sentience out and made them normal cupcakes once more.

"After that wailing, I feel pretty good about eating them." Raine picked up the frosting bag once more. "Does lavender work for everyone?"

"Sounds good to me."

"Save me one!"

Raine proceeded to take great pleasure in frosting the now silent cupcakes. Sara looked on with deep suspicion as she waited for them to talk again. Once they had all been frosted, everyone gathered around and selected one. Tori bit into hers with relish.

"These are perfect. Well done, girls."

Sara looked closely at hers. She still didn't feel entirely comfortable biting into it. Had it really been alive or was it some weird spell and nothing more?

Raine had no such qualms. She sank her teeth into the cupcake and smiled. The balance of lavender frosting to vanilla cupcake was perfect. Sara, however, would never look at a cupcake the same way again.

## CHAPTER THIRTY-FOUR

Tori looked at another batch of spoiled cupcakes. These were lumpy with a peculiar smell to them and she threw them out for the dragon to enjoy. She knew that he really enjoyed fresh meat, but a few cupcakes here and there were a nice treat.

Dorvu smelled them and flew down to investigate. He walked up to them and paused when one of them said.

"Mommy?"

The dragon tilted his head a little. He'd never heard of talking cupcakes before.

"Daddy?"

"Freedom!"

The dragon took a step closer and realized the cupcakes actually wriggled and tried to move toward him. Small bumps formed little faces. There was no denying that the cupcakes were, in fact, sentient and alive. Dorvu ushered the cupcakes toward him and looked around for something to carry them in. He couldn't leave them alone and defenseless. An old tablecloth with a hole in the corner caught the dragon's eye. He pulled it out of the bag that had been set out to go into the trash and took it over to the cupcakes. Carefully, he nosed them onto the fabric. Using his long claws, he bundled them together and lifted the parcel before he took off and looked for somewhere safe to keep them.

Dorvu hadn't met any other dragons, but his fatherly instincts had kicked in hard with the cupcakes. It didn't make sense from a natural point of view, but he didn't care about anything like that. He set them down carefully on a bed of moss in the middle of the woods near the teachers' cottages. He opened the tablecloth and looked more closely at his adopted offspring.

The cupcakes wriggled around and righted themselves.

"We're free!"

"No more frosting!"

"Now what?"

"I'm scared."

"Don't be scared." Dorvu nosed the cupcake he thought had said that. "I'll keep you safe."

---

Raine wandered through the woods and puzzled over something she'd read in one of her books when she came across the dragon watching over a tablecloth. She frowned and walked over.

"Good afternoon, Dorvu." She looked at the cupcakes. "What do you have there?"

"They're my adopted children."

She raised her eyebrow and jumped when one of the cupcakes turned its bumpy face toward her.

"Frosting woman!"

"She killed our brethren!"

"Murderer!"

"Lavender lover!"

"Dorvu…" Raine tried to think how to continue. "They're cupcakes."

"They're mine and I will raise them."

She sighed. This was not an argument she would easily win. "They're cakes that had a spell go slightly wrong."

"I will look after them and make sure they enjoy a fulfilling life."

Raine wasn't sure how to proceed. It wasn't something they really covered in Debate Club.

"They will grow stale and moldy after a few days. That would be a horrible death."

"No, we won't!"

"Lies!"

"You don't know what will happen." Dorvu guarded the cupcakes. "They should have a chance."

Raine squeezed the bridge of her nose. She didn't know how she would explain this to everyone else. She also didn't want to upset the dragon too much as she'd seen the effects of his icy breath.

"How will they live a good life? They can't move. They can't see. They don't eat or drink."

Dorvu crept closer to the cupcakes and guarded them more jealously with his body.

Raine put her hands up. "Okay. Enjoy your afternoon."

She turned and walked to the kitchen. Tori would not be happy with this development.

———

"So… Did you throw a batch of cupcakes out by any chance?" Raine put her hands in her pockets. "A batch that I made with Evie and Sara."

"Oh, don't be upset, dear." Tori gave her a motherly smile. "No one gets every batch perfect."

"Dorvu is guarding the cupcakes. They're talking." Raine sighed. "He's adopted them as though they're his children."

"Oh." The pixie deflated. "We'll have to tell the headmistress."

Raine squeezed her eyes shut. She could hear the conversation in her head, and it wasn't one she looked forward to having. Still, she went with Tori to the headmistress's office.

"Is everything okay?" Ms. Berens looked up from her notes. "The kitchen didn't get blown up, did it?"

"Ah, no. This is, well…" Tori shuffled her feet.

"We accidentally made sentient cupcakes and now, Dorvu has adopted them as his children." Raine pursed her lips together. "He is quite adamant about raising them."

The headmistress took a moment to process this news. She had never heard of sentient cupcakes before but wasn't too surprised to hear that the dragon had adopted them. He had shown strong protective instincts toward the students after all.

"I will speak to Horace and see if we can't resolve this

little problem." The headmistress stood. "Tell me, how exactly did they become sentient?"

"Sara's magic was mixed into the spell. We didn't realize it would act weirdly." Raine chewed her bottom lip. "Tori said it's the trickster nature of kitsune magic."

The headmistress nodded. She hadn't dealt with many kitsunes, but she had done a lot of reading on them in case Sara needed her help at some stage.

"I will speak to Horace. Thanks for bringing this to my attention."

---

"It itches!"

The dragon had put some of his magic into the cupcakes in the hopes of giving them more freedom and ability to live a life. They had complained of itching for the last twenty minutes. He huffed and bundled the tablecloth a little closer around them to try to make them more comfortable.

Horace was surprised to see Mara approach him. "Is everything okay?" The groundskeeper stood from his bench. "I don't often see you here."

"Well, I hope things aren't too bad. Dorvu has adopted a batch of sentient cupcakes."

Horace raised an eyebrow. "Let's see what we can do, then."

Not much concerned or got a rise out of the groundskeeper. He was one of the very few humans at the school, but he'd seen and heard it all. Or so he'd thought. This was a new one, even for him.

They walked through the woods to Dorvu's favorite sleeping place. The silver dragon lay curled around a wriggling tablecloth which he cooed over.

"What do you have there, Dorvu?" Horace called.

"Cupcakes. I added some of my magic into them."

Mara groaned. This was going from bad to worse.

A cupcake burst from the tablecloth with a pair of tiny silver wings. It giggled and cried out, "I'm free!"

The rest were close behind it with small silver wings of their own. Dorvu looked at them with the pride of a doting parent. The cupcakes wobbled but fluttered their small wings with great determination. They set out toward the river and the dragon watched with a blissful expression.

Mara, however, had a better idea of how this would end. She followed them to the water where they began to tire. They had no muscles to power the wings, and being cupcakes, there wasn't space for a lot of magic. They began to drop into the river where they gurgled and whined.

Dorvu walked over and watched with concern on his face as the cupcakes sank beneath the water. They bobbed back to the surface without a sound. He nudged one with his nose and received no response. To Mara's surprise, he swallowed the cupcake whole, and then the next.

"I thought they were your adopted children?" She looked at him, aghast. "You ate them."

The dragon shrugged as best as he could. "They were no longer alive and I saw no reason to waste perfectly good cupcakes."

CHAPTER THIRTY-FIVE

Raine groaned and pulled the blankets over her head. Something was happening outside, but it was far too early to be awake, let alone actually think. She shoved the blankets back down after a moment to wake fully. The lights flickered outside although it was the dead of night. Darkness stretched over the grounds, pierced by the few lights that remained on.

She hopped out of bed and looked out the window to see the lights dimming almost entirely before returning to half-light again. A chill ran down her spine. Something was very wrong. She could feel it.

The dragon swooped and snapped his teeth at the first intruder. The wizard pressed his magic against the boundary wards around the school grounds. He ignored the large creature entirely, which aggravated Dorvu even more. The dragon rose higher and gathered a big, deep breath. He dive-bombed the man and blew a great blast of icy air at him.

The trespasser froze on the spot. Small crystals of white frost formed over his skin and he was locked into position with his wand held up and a small crease between his brows. Dorvu landed and stalked around the edge of the grounds in search of the rest of them. He knew they were there to test the school's protection.

Raine walked into the hallway and padded softly down toward the main front door. She paused at the top of the stairs and listened as Professor Hudson, Professor Powell, and the headmistress talked in low voices.

"They must be the same people who walked onto the grounds to speak to Adrien." Mara sighed. "I did not expect them to be so determined."

"His parents said they weren't a real concern." Xander looked toward the stairs. "They shouldn't be too difficult to drive off."

"Dorvu sounds as though he's having some fun with them." Mara smiled. "I'm tempted to let him deal with them."

"We should strengthen the barriers while the dragon toys with them." Xander stepped out the door into the cool night. "The parents will never forgive us if anything happens to another student."

Mara knew he was right. There had been some pressure to bring another agent onto the school grounds, but she had soothed the parents' minds. Agent Connor was already out in the darkness, trying to apprehend whoever was poking at the boundary wards. Mara felt they were no real threat, but she wanted to be sure.

Xander strode out into the darkness and felt a thrill run through him. This was the first time he'd had a good reason to use his magic like this in a good while. As much as he enjoyed teaching the talented students of the school, there were times when he missed a more active role in the magical community. He wrapped shadow around himself to better sneak up on the intruders.

According to what they could feel from the wards, six people were positioned at various places around the grounds, trying to break in. They kept moving and testing with different forms of magic. Xander had chosen to take the front gates. They stretched skyward in the darkness and cast warped shadows from the dim lights nearby. The professor kept to the shadows. For him to walk down the main driveway through the light while wrapped in shadow would have given the game away.

An older woman crouched near the gates with her hands up and palms pressed against the wards. Her eyes were closed in concentration. A pulse of magic ran through the wards and the outer layer shivered under her pressure. They had made a little progress, which meant it was time for him to end this experimentation.

Xander whispered under his breath and formed a curse in his mind. It wouldn't kill her, but it would wipe her memory of anything related to the school. He flicked his hand and sent the magic through his wand to the woman. Her jaw dropped, and her eyes flew open. She walked away down the road as though controlled by an outside force. He saw her get into her car and drive away without a word.

---

Raine was unsure what to do next. She didn't have enough

control over her magic to help the teachers with the intruders but hated sitting there and doing nothing. With a deep sigh of frustration, she turned and returned to her room. There was no reason to make things worse. She'd do some research into the school wards the following day and tell Adrien what had happened in the morning.

She couldn't sleep as she saw the lights flicker and dim outside the window. There was no doubt that the teachers could handle it, but she itched to be good enough to help them. Soon, she reminded herself. She had improved, but she wouldn't put someone at risk for the sake of her ego.

---

Dorvu flew high enough in the sky that he wouldn't be seen from the ground thanks to the cloud cover and dimmed lights. The dragon thoroughly enjoyed this game. He usually hunted small prey, but these elves and wizards proved to be far more fun. They were sneakier and required him to try harder. The dragon considered whether he could get the students to play hide and seek with him.

Mara crept toward an older man who hummed a tune around his spell. The dragon watched as she zapped him with a particularly strong stun spell. The man dropped to the ground and Dorvu wheeled away to look for someone else to freeze.

Xander had found the dragon's first victim, but Dorvu found his next. A middle-aged elf with greying hair tried to scramble up a tree and climb over the wards. The dragon swooped in low and frosted the air around the tree. The man threw a spell at him, but he was too slow. Dorvu was gone before the spell could get anywhere near him.

He continued to swoop in and play with the elf. He knew the interloper wouldn't be able to climb over the wards, but he enjoyed taking his time to irritate him.

When the dragon next glided in, the man foolishly tried to jump on his back. Dorvu obliged and turned to let him land there. The elf gripped tightly and the dragon flapped his wings and soared high into the sky where he rolled and showed his belly to the stars.

The elf fell with a piercing scream before he landed with a thud and never made another sound. Dorvu felt particularly pleased with himself about that one.

Xander found the crumpled remains of the man the dragon had dropped from a great height. Horace was already on his way across the grounds with a wheelbarrow. The groundskeeper had disposed of a number of bodies during his service to the school and was familiar with the process.

"Is this the last one?" Horace pulled to a stop next to Xander. "I found the frozen one."

"This is the last." Xander smiled. "Thank you for your help."

"Don't worry. Are the wards standing strong?" Horace hauled the body into the barrow. "No holes?"

"No holes. They're exactly as they should be." The professor turned away. "We strengthened a few spots, but no one will gain entry to the grounds tonight."

# CHAPTER THIRTY-SIX

"Mom and Dad will be pissed." Etienne leaned against the doorframe. "Brace yourself."

Adrien rolled his eyes and picked up the phone. His parents had called to talk about the fact that someone from a rival family had tried to kidnap him—or, at the very least, bring him round to their way of thinking. Of course, they hadn't stood a chance. Adrien was loyal to his family and friends.

The phone rang twice before his father picked up.

"Adrien?"

"Hey, Dad."

"I have been informed that people from the Raven clan have tried to recruit you."

The young elf slumped down onto his bed.

"It's not that big a deal. They showed up at the school grounds and said their spiel. I said I wasn't interested."

"They tried to break through the wards yesterday."

Adrien sighed. This was going about as well as he had expected.

"You sent me here because it has some of the most talented teachers and the best track record."

"I am aware of why I sent you there, Adrien. That does not change the fact that I am concerned about your safety."

"I'm fine. There's nowhere safer."

He could picture his father's face in his mind, complete with the deep frown and hard eyes.

"You will tell me the moment you see those people again."

"I won't see them again."

"I'll send Marcel to watch over things."

Adrien held back a groan. Marcel was a killjoy. "Dad, seriously. I'm safe here. They even have a dragon watching the grounds."

He had heard that the dragon had killed the attempted intruders.

"Fine. If anything slightly suspicious happens, I will send Marcel."

"Okay, Dad."

"Take care and keep your grades up."

His dad hung up and Adrien dropped the phone onto his bed.

"So it went that well, huh?" Etienne walked into the room. "How mad was he?"

"Not too bad. He tried to send Marcel."

Etienne shook his head. "Marcel would insist we give up Louper and try to enforce a curfew."

Adrien lay back on his bed. "He said I have to tell him the moment something suspicious happens."

"Will you?"

"Define suspicious..." He grinned, and his older brother laughed. "Don't worry. I'm sure they'll have given up now."

"Don't be late for practice later."

"I wouldn't miss it for the world."

Etienne left Adrien to his thoughts. He was entirely unconcerned by the attempts of the Raven clan to try to tempt him to their side.

# CHAPTER THIRTY-SEVEN

Raine looked in the mirror, pleased with the result. She'd put her hair up into a French braid and Sara had woven a daisy into it. Cameron had finally managed to find a little time where they could be alone together and she was nervous as she had never been on a date before. She really liked him and didn't want to lose his friendship if she screwed something up.

"It'll be amazing. Cameron is a sweetheart." Sara hugged her gently. "Go and have fun."

They planned to take a nice walk through the woods on the grounds and watch the sun set behind the mountains. Raine took a steadying breath and left the safety of her room to go and meet Cameron.

He had dressed in his best pair of jeans and a dark button-down shirt that brought out the color of his eyes. Raine smiled, he looked very handsome as he approached her with a bright smile.

"You look beautiful." He held his arm out for her to take. "I've looked forward to this all week."

She hooked her arm around his and they strolled out onto the school grounds. They had roughly an hour until sunset.

"Have you found anything interesting to study in the library this week?" Cameron looked at her. "You always look so vibrant when you find a particularly fascinating subject."

Raine felt her cheeks heat at the compliment. "I looked into the history of Aztec iconography and its usage in modern magic." She chewed on her bottom lip. "The old translations are mostly lost to time, but there are some covens of witches who do use the old iconography. It is often mixed in with Aztec."

"That does sound fascinating." He led her off the main path and onto the soft grass. "Do these witches follow the old Aztec ways with blood and all?"

"Not normally. There were a few notes and suggestions that some did, but those were dark witches. The library doesn't have anything about dark magic in it." Raine glanced at Cameron and saw the way the light struck his jawline. "I don't blame them, but I am really curious."

"I like to study the theory of it all. I look into the ancient ways sometimes when I want to lose myself in something else." He shifted his direction slightly to approach the woods. "Have you read any good fiction books recently?"

"I haven't had much time for fiction. There are so many good non-fiction books." She looked down and away. "You?"

Raine enjoyed Cameron's company but she wasn't sure if this was going well. She was happy and liked being close to him, but she wasn't sure whether she perhaps bored him. Should she try to move the conversation onto some of his interests?

"I read a great thriller. I finished it last night." He tried to steady his racing heart. "It was one of those treasure hunting ones where they travel the world to find the mysterious artifact."

"Oh, that sounds fun!" Raine relaxed a little. "You'll have to give me the title when I have a little more time."

Cameron wanted to get to know more about her. He knew what she shared with their friendship group, but he wanted to really know her.

"Do you have any movies you want to see or anything?" He ground his teeth, frustrated at how lame that sounded. "I mean, there are a bunch of cool movies coming out soon."

"There's a superhero one that looks really fun." Raine smiled. "Do you know the one I mean?"

"Yeah. That does look awesome." Cameron tried to think of a better topic of conversation, something that would make her smile. "You did martial arts, right?"

"I started when I could walk. My dad and uncle wanted to make sure that I could look after myself. It really helped my confidence too." She brushed a branch out of her way. "What about you? Have you done martial arts?"

"I studied capoeira. I've kept my training up in the evenings here, but I'll return to full lessons over the summer. I'm thinking about inviting William along." He had looked forward to lessons again. "Tell me more about yourself. I really want to get to know you, but I'm at a loss as to what to say."

They arrived at a small mossy bank overlooking the river. They sat close to one another and Cameron put his arm around Raine's shoulders.

"I'm not sure what to say." She laughed. "I'm in the same boat as you."

They both chuckled at that and felt better for admitting that they were each as lost as the other.

"When I was younger, I used to get in trouble with Uncle Jerry because he'd catch me hiding under the blankets and reading until past midnight." She smiled. "He eventually gave up and realized I loved books far more than sleep."

Cameron laughed. "My parents reached the same conclusion. I haven't had much time to really read like I did back home, but I love curling up with a good book." He squeezed her shoulders. "I'm happy in my life, but there's something to be said for experiencing an adventure you'll never have yourself. You know?"

"Yes, exactly." She leaned her head on his shoulder. "I'll never fly through space and meet six-armed aliens or discover a world at the center of Earth. It's fun escaping into a book where I can do stuff like that, though."

"Is it weird that I love fantasy?" He stroked her hair tenderly. "I mean, I'm a shifter. For a lot of those authors, my existence is fantasy."

"No, I think it's cool. I love fantasy too. In a weird way, it's relaxing and comforting." Raine sighed contentedly. "It's also interesting to see the way humans approach those topics."

"I think fantasy can be a fantastic tool to help integrate magicals and humans too." Cameron shifted his weight a little. "It gives both sides a safe space to explore their relationship with each other."

"I completely agree!" She turned to face him. "Maybe we could work on that and even speak to some authors. I'm sure the government would be on board."

He stroked his thumb along her cheek and gazed into her eyes.

"You come alive when you talk like that. Your eyes glitter like stars and your entire being comes to life." He leaned in a little. "I have never seen someone quite so passionate and alive as you before."

Raine leaned into him. She'd never been kissed before, but she felt as though she was ready and he was the right guy. Neither of them spoke as they inched closer until their lips brushed lightly. She found his lips to be soft and pliant and feeling brave, leaned in and kissed him properly. Butterflies exploded in her stomach and her cheeks heated as they kissed softly for the first time.

Cameron held her close and gave her all the time she needed. She looked into his eyes and kissed him again, a little harder this time. Her fear slowly melted away to be replaced with the happiness and pleasure of feeling his lips against hers. She hoped she never forgot that moment, that first time.

# CHAPTER THIRTY-EIGHT

"You guys kissed?" Sara took Raine's hands and sat down on her bed. "Tell me everything."

Raine blushed and sat beside her. Evie climbed onto Sara's bed and tucked her legs under her.

"Was it really romantic?" Evie grinned at her. "It was, wasn't it?"

Raine smiled. "We walked and talked, mostly about books. He's so sweet and kind. We have a similar interest in books too, and we can talk martial arts. We sat near the river and everything felt right, so we kissed. It was perfect." She grinned. "It really was like something out of the movies. His lips are soft, and he was gentle."

Sara pretended to swoon. "You guys are so good together." She hugged Raine. "You're adorable and you're a great influence on each other."

Raine and Sara turned to Evie.

"Now." Sara squeezed Evie's hand. "When will you kiss William?"

Evie sighed. "I want to, but I don't think he's ready." She shrugged. "I won't rush him into anything. He's so shy when it comes to things like this. I think I'll need to make the move when the time's right."

"We're modern women so there's nothing wrong with that." Sara beamed at Evie. "William comes to life when he's around you, though. He was this quiet, grumpy thing when we first met him, but around you, he's a total sweetie."

"I really like him. I hate that he had a bad start in life, but he has a heart of gold." Evie lay back on the bed. "I know he'll be the most incredible man."

"He's going into the FBI like you, isn't he, Raine?" Sara looked at Raine. "I'm sure I heard him mention that."

"I think so. He would make an awesome agent." Raine turned to Evie. "You guys could settle together. You could run your bakery or your potions store, and he could be an agent. You'll both make the world a little brighter."

Evie wrinkled her nose.

"We haven't even kissed yet. I don't want to plan my life with him." She stretched her legs. "That seemed like it'd jinx it. So much could happen. I want to enjoy each day as it comes."

"Wiser words were never spoken." Sara nodded. "I'm not really ready to date. I had the biggest crush on Adrien's brother Etienne for about a week, but I don't think I'm ready for all that. I have too much other stuff going on."

"How do you feel about your kitsune magic?" Raine squeezed Sara's hand. "Is it coming on okay?"

Sara shrugged. "I guess. I don't know."

"Do you want to talk about it?" Evie sat up and put her

arm around Sara's shoulders. "We're here for you, you know that, right?"

"Yeah." Sara hugged her friends. "I'd be lost without you guys. I don't know what I did to deserve such amazing friends."

"Like attracts like," Raine responded with another hug. "You're one of the most amazing people I've ever met."

"Agreed." Evie scrabbled under her bed and pulled out a bag of M&Ms. "This feels like a good time to break into the M&Ms stash."

She passed the bag to Raine and Sara.

"Sometimes, it feels like I need to have my whole life planned out even though I'm not entirely sure what I'm doing tomorrow." Sara popped an M&M into her mouth. "You know?"

"There can be a lot of pressure to have this complicated map of how everything will come together, but we're only freshmen," Raine agreed. "I feel like there should be a heavier focus on enjoying life."

"I completely agree." Evie nodded and helped herself to a handful of M&Ms. "We only have one life and sometimes, it feels like we're expected to pack it full of work and 'meaningful' stuff. I mean, who decides what's meaningful anyway? And so what if we need to spend a day cloud-gazing or something? What is so wrong with wandering for a little while and figuring it all out as we go along?"

"I have no idea. The obsession with boxes and plans is exhausting." Sara picked out the blue M&Ms. "My family are dying for me to put my plan of action out from now until I'm thirty."

"I'm so lucky that Uncle Jerry simply wants me to be

happy," Raine said quietly. "I couldn't live with that pressure."

"My family isn't so bad but it can be a lot sometimes." Sara shrugged. "It'll be easier once I come into my kitsune magic."

"You'll get there. I know it." Evie smiled. "And we'll help you every step of the way."

## CHAPTER THIRTY-NINE

The stealth spell popped around the friends, but Raine barely noticed. She looked around her slowly. Something felt off. Cameron stood stiff and alert and his instincts told him something was wrong. A soft whisper passed through the shoppers around them. Raine was aware of furtive glances in their direction. Could someone have told the teachers they had sneaked down there?

Philip walked with his head high and led the group down the small path to their right. He was aware of the gazes and the odd quietness that wrapped around them but chose to ignore it rather than let it get to him.

The shifter's protective instincts kicked into overdrive. He remained alert as he moved to the back of the group to try to protect them from any incoming attacks. William moved to walk beside Philip. He kept his wand in his hand and his fire magic coursed through his veins.

Raine walked beside Cameron and watched everyone

who passed them at a slower pace than usual. A Willen narrowed her eyes at them before she scurried down a narrow alleyway leading into darkness. The atmosphere eased as they walked deeper into the kemana and people paid more attention to their shopping. Raine relaxed a little but still watched for suspicious activity.

They discovered a shop that sold all sorts of weird and interesting candies, cakes, and sodas. Evie spotted the licorice cola from the window and they had to go and investigate from there. Raine and Cameron were drawn to the cakes. Each was cupcake-sized with intricate decorations. She wasn't sure how someone could have such a steady hand as to create the lace-looking icing on top of the lavender and elderflower cake.

The nettle cake didn't sound appealing, though. She had heard of nettle tea, but it didn't sound like something that would do well in a cake. A gin and tonic cake sounded like something she thought Agent Connor might like. She made a mental note of where the shop was so she could pick up some things when they were officially allowed down there.

Sara made a beeline for the candies. "Oh, wow! They have pancakes and maple syrup jelly beans." She pulled out her wallet to see how many Ruby Falls coins she had. "Those were created just for me."

Evie wrinkled her nose at the bacon mints. She wasn't sure why people insisted on adding bacon to everything. She liked it for breakfast, but bacon mints were two steps too far. The habanero hard candies and pickle candy canes were a hard no too. She paused when she saw the cinnamon candies, and her face lit up when she spotted the violet gummies. Those were something she could very much enjoy. Evie felt that violet was one of those flavors that was drastically overlooked. Many people complained that it tasted like perfume, but she absolutely adored it.

The price wasn't bad, so she bought a large bag of the violet gummies to eat while she was studying. The group returned to the street outside. Sara looked at Evie's gummies with an expression of intense confusion.

"You eat violet?"

Evie laughed. "You can, yes."

"It's not used often, but it's like lavender." Adrien smiled. "You can eat a lot of flowers. People merely choose not to. Rosewater, for example, adds a very nice touch to a lot of delicate cakes and cookies."

Cameron caught it first—the harsh whisper of someone saying Adrien's name and some sharp words. His ears shifted into wolf ears to listen better.

"Didn't know that was a thing." Evie nodded at his ears. "Partial shifts, interesting."

Raine looked in the direction his ears pointed. A pair of older witches whispered and looked at the group. She was sorely tempted to walk over to them and demand to know what was going on. Fortunately, she knew better than that and gripped her wand a little tighter as she called her magic.

The group closed ranks and walked close together as they all glanced around for any sign of trouble.

"Should we go back to school and do this another day?" Evie glanced over her shoulder. "Things feel really weird here today."

"No." Adrien glared at the witches who still whispered

together. "We won't give in that easily."

They had no particular destination in mind and were there simply to explore and see what cool new things they found. That was, after all, how they'd found Bubble and Fizz. Slowly, the group relaxed as the witches were left behind them and they spotted a crepe stand.

"Crepes sound really good." Sara gestured to the stand. "Who wants one?"

"Strawberries and Nutella sounds heavenly." Evie walked up to the stand. "William, would you like one?"

"I'd love one." He remained on guard. "Thank you."

Evie ordered everyone a strawberry and Nutella crepe. She was aware of the tension they all felt but tried to enjoy the kemana regardless. They wouldn't let those people, whoever they were, ruin the experience for them.

She handed everyone their crepe which they ate with great relish. Adrien smiled as he enjoyed a piece of home. He thought about talking to the pixies to see if they would mind letting him have crepes for breakfast. They were easy to make but he didn't want to make their lives more difficult. They had been generous with their foods so far.

"Why don't we head left?" Sara pointed to a street with purple lighting. "It looks arty and interesting."

No one had any argument with that, so they followed her down the street with lilac and royal-purple lights hanging overhead.

A large swarm of butterflies in blood-reds and emerald-greens appeared from nowhere and gathered around the group to block them from the view of the rest of the street. Raine held her wand in her hand and looked around for an attacker. Cameron remained close to her side, shifted partially, and bared his lupine teeth. Adrien felt the shift in magic.

The butterflies began to hum. The deep thrum blocked out any other sound. The group tried to remain close together, but they lost sight of each other. The shifter remained glued to Raine's side, but she couldn't see the others. Adrien summoned his sword when he realized that he had been separated from his friends. He had trained for situations like this. The magic in the butterflies felt sticky to his senses and blocked his hearing. He quieted his mind and tried to feel out anyone who might be nearby.

The elf planted his feet and waited. He knew they would make their move soon. They had to. A sharp pain bloomed in his lower back and the elf spun to face his attacker. He saw nothing but a wall of red and green in constant motion. His head spun and his vision blurred. Whatever the pain had been included poison, or at least a potion.

Adrien fought to remain on his feet, but it felt as though the ground swayed beneath him. His muscles no longer obeyed his commands. Darkness closed in and swallowed his vision and he lost consciousness.

Strong arms caught the young elf. The butterflies dissipated in time for Raine to see a tall, broad man with close-cropped red hair step through a small portal with Adrien limp in his arms. She called her magic but there was no spell she knew that would help him. William called his fire and threw a fireball at the man with the aim to make him pause long enough to do something more. Cameron dodged the fireball and lunged at the man, but he was too slow.

The portal closed with a soft pop. Raine was filled with a rage. How dare they take her friend from her?

# CHAPTER FORTY

Raine raced into the library, followed by the others. Several students paused to watch her with confusion on their faces before the whispers started as they speculated as to what was wrong with her. She slowed her pace to a speedy walk as she headed toward the spells section. The library had become a home away from home and she had a good idea about where to find what they were after.

They needed a location spell to find Adrien and get him back. She'd read about them during her studies on portals and spells. Whoever had taken the elf—Raine was quite sure it was the rival family that had harassed him—had used a portal. That made life far more difficult, which Raine knew was the reason why they'd done it.

There was a small chance they were hundreds of miles away, but she didn't think they had that kind of magic. She wasn't sure why she thought that. Perhaps there was something about the way the portal had formed. There must have been something she'd read or heard in the past. It didn't matter now. They needed to get Adrien back.

The group spread out down the aisle and skimmed the titles on the spines of the books in search of something that might relate to a location spell. Raine chewed her bottom lip. She'd spent a lot of time in this library but that particular spell type evaded her. Of course, she knew they existed, and she also knew they tended to be complicated, but that wouldn't stop them.

The head librarian sighed softly. Raine and her friends were in some kind of trouble and that concerned him. They had all proven themselves to be dedicated students with excellent records. The way they had rushed into the library with almost wild looks on their faces and raced directly to the spell section told him they were in magical trouble. He strolled up to Raine. His poppy growled as he approached her. She turned to face him with a tight smile. That wasn't like her at all. She was usually bright and happy to see him. His stomach sank.

"Is everything okay?" Librarian Decker asked her. "You seem troubled."

Raine frowned, a deep expression that filled her eyes and formed crinkles at the corners of her mouth. He knew then that everything was far from okay. He wouldn't let her go through whatever it was alone. The gnome had developed a large soft spot for her over the months.

A little uncomfortable, she looked around. She had grown to trust the head librarian. He had been very kind to her and devoted much time to help her with her magic.

Time was ticking. Every moment they spent looking for the spell was time that they could and should use to save Adrien. Who knew what they were doing to him? She bit her bottom lip, made her decision, and spoke in a low, calm voice.

"I'm afraid that we're in trouble. Someone kidnapped Adrien. We were in the kemana—I know we shouldn't be there, but we had to explore. And we believe it was someone from a rival family. They escaped in a portal. He was unconscious."

The gnome's jaw tightened. He had suspected they'd sneaked into the kemana but that was a normal freshmen thing to do and he let that go. The kidnapping, however, was a far bigger problem, one the students wouldn't be able to solve on their own.

"I will make you and your friends a deal." He looked sternly at the group. "I will help you find your friend on the condition that both Joe and I accompany you on the trip to bring him back. We will not tell the headmistress until we return."

Raine nodded enthusiastically. The head librarian watched as the other students thought about it before they also nodded.

Satisfied with the outcome, he found the book they needed. He had performed the spell before, but he thought the students would benefit from the guide. Joe heard his name and came over to see what was going on. Librarian Decker filled him in quickly and Joe rushed off to ensure the other gnomes covered for them while they did what needed to be done.

The head librarian led the group into his private study off the library. The door was a simple dark wood one which almost blended in with the surrounding bookshelves. He didn't want anyone to interrupt his peace while he was in there and preferred it to be at least slightly hidden.

Raine looked around the room and smiled at how it reflected the gnome's personality. Books lined every wall and his broad desk was heaped with more books and papers. At first glance, it looked chaotic, but she could discern his organizational system when she looked more closely. A dark-yellow light hung from the ceiling and cast deep shadows in the corners and around the bottom of the bookshelves. She would have loved to explore the tomes there but it wasn't the time.

"This is a complicated spell and we need to cast it now." He opened the book and placed it on the desk in front of them. "I have everything we need. Read through the instructions while I set up the runes and candles."

Raine read through the spell instructions and tried to break it down into images she could call during the actual casting. It had a few steps they needed to work through as a unified group. She called her magic and pushed it into her wand in preparation. Cameron put his arm around her shoulders and leaned his head against hers.

"What can I do?"

Librarian Decker looked at the shifter. "Don't you worry. Merely say the words along with us. Your shifter magic will help the spell along. You can't actively use it, but the spell will call upon it."

Cameron relaxed once he felt he could play a role in

this. His lack of magic hadn't concerned him at all until that moment. He wanted to get his friend back. Adrien was the quiet, reserved one of the group but the shifter had developed a deep respect for the elf. He had shown a strong sense of honor and loyalty, and he appreciated that in him.

Librarian Decker marked the runes on the floor and placed the candles near them. The last time he had used this spell was to find his brother. To his surprise, his brother had been hiding in the attic reading the latest book from his favorite author. He remembered that he had felt a mixture of relieved, frustrated, and delighted.

Raine studied the complicated markings on the floor and ran the words of the spell through her mind. She was confident in her pronunciation, but everything had to be precise. This wasn't a small tracker spell like they used in Louper. This was a large, complicated working to locate someone potentially hundreds of miles away.

The students stepped into the middle circle and spread to stand an equal distance from one another. The gnome stood at the head of the proceedings beneath the angular rune that would form the actual tracker.

He led the spell and began each round of spoken words with a confidence and clarity that filled Raine with hope and assurance that they would get Adrien back. She felt her magic flow into the runes and smiled as they began to glow a bright white. The head librarian's voice increased in volume as they began the final piece of the spell.

Cameron felt an odd tugging sensation as something flowed from his navel into the rune behind him. His magic had never been used for anything other than shifting before, and he had no way to use it for anything other than his transformation. Such was the way of the shifter. It had not bothered him at all, but that sensation was one he'd rather not repeat if he had a choice.

A brilliant white orb appeared in the middle of the circle with a fizzing sound. It turned a pale blue and the gnome breathed a sigh of relief. That meant Adrien was within fifty miles of their location. The orb buzzed and bounced as it urged them to follow it.

Joe stepped into the room and gave his colleague a small nod. The arrangements had been made to watch over the library and the headmistress would be given a suitable excuse for their absence. They walked to the large dark bookshelf behind the desk and Joe pulled on a slender green book.

The bookshelf moved away from the wall and creaked slowly outward to reveal a dark corridor. Orange orbs bloomed into existence at regular intervals along the bare stone walls. They cast enough light for them to walk with confidence. Raine smiled and hoped she would have a chance to explore the other hidden passages and rooms of the school.

"We can't allow anyone to see us leave. There would be too many questions." The head librarian stepped into the corridor. "We must hurry."

They followed the orb down the corridor at a brisk jog and no one dared say a word. After a short while, they emerged behind the main school and not too far from the kitchens. Evie glanced over and hoped the pixies wouldn't see them. They'd ask so many questions. The two gnomes led them to their respective cars, and the students divided into two groups. Raine, Cameron, and Sara went with Leo. Philip, Evie, and William went with Joe.

The orb remained with Librarian Decker and he led the way down the driveway and out into the countryside. Raine kept her wand in her hand. They would get Adrien back.

# CHAPTER FORTY-ONE

Adrien groaned. He rubbed his temples and slowly opened his eyes. It took a moment to adjust to the low light levels and focus on where he was. He was surrounded by cold grey stone. Thick metal bars formed a wall in front of him. The gaps between them were too small for him to try to squeeze between them, and the bars were too thick to try to bend them with his magic. He pushed himself into a sitting position and tried to look for a way out.

There was stone all around him apart from the bars, which revealed a stone corridor. He placed his hand against the cool rock beneath him, closed his eyes, and allowed his magic to flow into the stone. It was far too thick for him to work with, and earth magic had never been his strong suit to begin with. He took a slow breath and shifted his focus onto his body to search for injuries or foreign magic. When he felt nothing but a couple of bruises, he relaxed.

Adrien stood and walked around the large cell. It was some ten feet by ten feet, which gave him plenty of room to walk and stretch. He ran his fingertips over the wall and allowed his magic through them to try to feel something that would give him an advantage. There was nothing, not even a clue about his whereabouts. Frustration bubbled up within him. He wouldn't sit there and wait for Raine and everyone to rescue him. Or even worse, his brother. He'd never live it down if Etienne came to rescue him.

He moved to the bars and reached out to touch them, but his body rebelled. Adrien narrowed his eyes before he smiled. The bars were an illusion. It was a good one that came with the magic to discourage people from touching it. He needed to unravel the illusion. That gave him something to focus on. Professor Powell had taught them how to work through illusions recently.

The elf sat cross-legged on the floor and closed his eyes to focus better on his magic and the illusion before him. His power erupted into a wildfire within him and he smiled. He pressed it gently against the illusion and began to feel methodically for the edges of it. At first, his magic reacted like his body had and refused to make contact with the illusion. Adrien pushed harder and finally felt the cool, glassy sensation of the enchantment.

He kept his breathing slow and steady as he began at the floor and spread his magic along until he found the final thread where the illusion met the wall. He tugged on it with his own power and felt the glassiness begin to crack. The elf smiled and tugged harder as he pushed his magic around the rest of the illusion in search of the other edges. He tugged on the first thread near the left wall and soon found the next one near the ceiling. Carefully, he wrapped his magic around it and began to tug on that one too.

When he found the third and finally, the fourth edge, the glassiness of the illusion began to turn to soft sand. He had made good progress. Had he opened his eyes, he would have seen the bars before him shimmer and ripple like someone had thrown stones into a pond. He tugged and pulled on the threads and ignored the increasing weariness that came over him. Adrien had trained since he could walk to deal with situations like these, and a little tiredness wouldn't stop him.

Suddenly, the entire illusion gave and turned into an odd snow-blizzard sensation as each piece of the illusion melted when it hit the floor. He opened his eyes and sighed. The bars were gone but he now faced a simple corridor of an older building. The wall before him was a dirty cream color and cobwebs hung from the corner where the ceiling met the wall. The floor was a dust-coated wooden floor that must have been beautiful in its prime. A rich reddish color could be seen beneath some of the thinner patches of dirt and grime.

Adrien stood and composed himself. He was one step closer to escape. A muffled voice came from somewhere to his right. He walked out of the room and realized he was in some form of converted basement. The voice grew louder, and he found another cell like his own. It contained a younger boy with large pale-blue eyes and a mop of pale-blonde hair. Adrien saw the tips of his ears and wondered which guardian family he had been stolen from.

The boy looked to be around about ten, too young to

have really mastered his magic. Adrien pushed aside his tiredness and made short work of the illusion holding the young elf in place. He extended his hand and smiled softly. He would return him to his family.

"What's your name?"

The elf boy looked at him wide-eyed before he gathered himself and stood tall as a guardian should.

"Rafe."

Adrien smiled. He noted the Bordeaux accent on the boy. That would help to return him home safely. "I'm Adrien. I'll get you home to your family. Tell me, Rafe, how long have you been here?"

Rafe took a tentative step closer to Adrien. "I'm not sure. They've fed me twice. They say my family is evil and they'll train me for the righteous path."

Adrien resisted the urge to roll his eyes. He had been warned about those who had left the true guardian path in favor of glory and money.

"Come. We'll get out of here and go home."

Rafe smiled and took his hand. The older elf studied the spacious cellar around them. There was only one way in and out. The rickety wooden stairs had seen better days, but they looked as though they wouldn't collapse too soon. Adrien pursed his lips. There would likely be guards on the other side of the door at the top of those stairs. He formed his sword and held it out while he pushed Rafe behind him without releasing his hand.

"You're like my big sister." The youngster looked at Adrien in awe. "I haven't been given my sword yet."

"Do you have a dagger or any spells, Rafe?" Adrien led him to the stairs. "We'll need to fight our way out of here."

"I have a dagger." He called it quickly. "I know how to fight."

"I know you do." He smiled to reassure his brave companion. "You're a guardian like me."

Rafe filled with pride. He was the youngest of his siblings and they often looked down on him for being little, but he would be a brave guardian like his big sister and mom.

Adrien tested the bottom step. Satisfied that it didn't creak, he led their slow ascent up the stairs. They had no idea what waited for them on the other side of that door. He called his magic and formed a shield around himself and Rafe. The tiredness slowed his magic down, but he couldn't afford to give in to it. He might be able to steal a little food on his way out of the building they were kept in, which would help to restore his strength.

Rafe tensed behind him as Adrien released his hand and twisted the door handle. He peered through the crack as he opened the door. One guard sat almost asleep on a short wooden stool. The elf studied him quickly and decided a surprise attack would be best.

Adrien threw the door open and rushed the man. He hit him in the temple with a hard blow from the hilt of his sword which he followed up with a concussive spell. It wouldn't kill him, but he wouldn't wake up any time soon.

Rafe watched with a huge grin on his face as his older companion neutralized the guard before the man had any idea what had happened. The young boy thought he'd found a new hero. He followed closely behind Adrien with his dagger at the ready as they crept down the hallway toward the main part of the house. The young elf grew more confident that he'd be home by dinner time. This Adrien would make his mom proud.

# CHAPTER FORTY-TWO

The orb bounced in front of the head librarian's car and guided him toward the mountains and the dense forests. A stone formed in the pit of his stomach. He knew what resided in those forests, and it wasn't pleasant. Raine sat on the back seat with her fingers entwined with Cameron's. She held her wand tightly and watched the landscape fly past. They would get Adrien back safe and sound. There was no other possible outcome.

The gnome turned down a narrow road where the trees grew tall and dense around them. The sun was blocked out by increasingly thick foliage as the road narrowed further. The orb led them around a sharp turn and down a dirt track which came to an abrupt end. He turned the engine off and waited for Joe to pull up beside him before he got out. The students piled out of the cars with their wands at the ready and an eagerness in their eyes.

"Be careful. There are spells and traps in this forest. This isn't a game of Louper. You won't be returned to the field if you fall into one." The head librarian looked sternly at the group around him. "Watch out for each other and keep your magic at the ready. I recommend you take your wolf form, young shifter."

Cameron wasted no time. He nuzzled his face against Raine's hand before he took point in front of Librarian Decker. His shifter senses allowed him to see and feel things before the others. Raine walked with the head librarian with her magic at the surface, ready to be used if they needed it. A cold darkness seeped into the space around them and crept along the ground like a thin mist. Cameron curled his lip and his hackles rose as he felt an unnatural fear begin to fill him. His instincts screamed at him to turn and run. He bit at the mist but there was nothing but thin air.

Raine's fear came in the form of her mind suddenly filled with concerns about letting her friends down. The farther she walked into the forest, the more the images in her mind sharpened. It began with simple ideas of her friends leaving her due to disappointment. It progressed into gruesome images of their deaths caused by her incompetence or lack of magical ability. She straightened her spine, determined that she wouldn't be driven away by a simple fear spell.

The darkness closed in around them. They could taste it on their tongues now, old blood and acrid chemical tastes. Cameron shook his head and tried to clear his nose and mouth from the awful taste and smell. The head librarian felt as though the darkness closed in around him and crushed his chest. He knew what the spell was, but he wasn't sure how to destroy it. The enchantment spread through an expanse of forest which spoke of a talented wizard.

William took Evie's hand in his before he closed his eyes and called his fire. He stoked it into a raging inferno within him. It threatened to consume him, but he was a half-Ifrit and the fire was part of him. He opened his eyes and pushed it outward in a rolling wave of pure light and heat. It passed over his friends and left them entirely unharmed. The darkness burned and evaporated beneath his flames.

Relief flooded the group as the harsh fear left them. William wobbled, and Evie caught him. He'd never used such a huge amount of magic before and it had drained him. He swallowed hard and tried to stand upright again. Joe hurried to him and placed his hand on William's arm as he handed him a small bar of something that looked like chocolate.

"Eat this. It'll replenish your magic. I grabbed them while I prepared for our little adventure."

William stuffed the chocolate bar in his mouth in one huge bite and chewed. Evie held him steady as he swayed. Slowly, he began to feel stronger again and stood on his own. He leaned his head against hers and thanked her quietly.

"Thank you, Joe." William smiled at the gnome. "I really appreciate your foresight."

Joe patted him on the arm and they continued deeper into the forest. Evie kept her arm wrapped around William's. Cameron walked at the edge of the group and checked that everyone was okay before he returned to the point position. His protective instincts kicked in strongly. These were his friends, his adopted pack.

Raine heard something at the very edge of her hearing. At first, it sounded like the rustling of leaves but then it became a song. The soft melody brought a smile to her face and told her of beautiful days full of sunshine and laughter. Suddenly, she felt a gentle pressure on her hand and saw Cameron bite her hand and tug at her. She looked down hurriedly and realized she was about to step into a dark pool of water.

Librarian Decker hauled Philip back from the edge. Raine ground her teeth. She hated that a piece of magic had so easily taken hold of her. She rubbed behind Cameron's ears and hoped that it didn't come across as a condescending form of affection.

"Thank you." She smiled at him.

Evie looked around. The forest had changed from pine to birch and oak at some point. She ran to the closest birch tree and peeled some of its fine silver bark away. She tore it into equal strips and pressed some of her magic into it. This was something her grandmother had taught her when she was a little girl.

"This won't taste good but place it on your tongue. It'll help protect you." She handed everyone a piece. "Hold it on your tongue for ten minutes and press your magic into it as you do so."

She smiled at Cameron. "I think you'll be immune, but you can have a strip if you don't want to take the risk."

He opened his mouth. While he wasn't keen on eating bark, he'd give it a go if it helped him keep everyone safe.

Raine placed it on her tongue and was pleasantly

surprised. It wasn't a foul taste and was certainly earthy but bearable. She pushed her magic into it while visualizing protection and clarity. They continued their walk through the woods and remained alert and on guard.

The ground cleared, and the trees were now spaced farther apart. It seemed too easy after everything they'd been through. Raine removed the bark from her tongue and tossed it into a bush seconds before the final level of protection formed in front of them. Bright red eyes peered at them from between the trees. An entire wall of them had formed. The animals took a step forward and she saw large, muscular wolves with spikes running down their spine.

"They would have had a better chance if they'd made them look realistic." Raine drew on the spell professor Powell had taught them. "They're clearly illusions."

Cameron stood at her side with his teeth bared while the others formed a line with their wands up. The gnomes stood on either end, looks of grim determination on their faces. The head librarian knew that the illusions had been cast in a way that played with the mind of those who encountered them. If one of those wolves bit a student, they would gain the injury as though a real wolf had bitten them. Their body would work against them. He wouldn't let that happen.

Each student called upon their magic and worked through the process Professor Powell had taught them as the wolves charged. Raine stood strong and determined as she reached for the edges of the illusions. She knew they were there. Fear did not come. She was entirely confident in the abilities of herself and her friends. The gnomes had more experience and found the edges first. They tore at them with vicious ferocity and ripped the images of the wolves apart with brutal precision.

Cameron leaned his head against Raine's side when the wolves blinked out of existence. She was safe once more and now, they could see where Adrien was held.

The tracking orb hurtled forward toward an old mansion hidden deep in the forest. It had been built into the cliff face of a large rocky outcrop. The structure stood some three stories tall and sprawled through the woods. They would need to use everything they had to find their elf friend and get him out in time. Cameron sniffed the air and caught the scent of at least ten magic users. He knew three were elves, but he couldn't pin the others down. There was something wrong with them.

The group did not hesitate but moved determinedly toward the mansion. There was no time to spend walking the perimeter and plotting the best way to sneak in. They needed to get their friend back and would go in the front door with their wands blazing.

# CHAPTER FORTY-THREE

Adrien looked down the hallway in both directions and was surprised that there were no more guards. He grew increasingly suspicious as he led Rafe down the left hallway and still didn't see or hear anyone. It began to feel like a trap. He paused to listen at the door on his right and heard nothing inside. When he rattled the door handle, he found it locked. He'd been taught how to pick a lock, but it didn't seem like a good idea.

They continued to the end of the hallway and emerged in a larger room with windows that looked out over a small garden with a large forest at its edges. Adrien held up his hand when Rafe moved to walk into the room. There had to be a reason why they hadn't bumped into their captors yet. He poked the tip of his sword into the room and felt the magic there. Footsteps raced toward the room from the hallway on the far side.

The elf sighed and looked over his shoulder as he tried

to decide whether it would be better to fight or look for a way out in the other direction. Rafe held his dagger, ready to fight. Adrien took the boy's hand and ran in the opposite direction. He wasn't ready to risk injury to his young companion or worse, being in a fight against who knew how many magic users.

They skidded around a corner and ducked into a small room with peeling pale-blue wallpaper and a tall, thin window at the far side. It was too narrow for Adrien to fit through, but Rafe might be able to. The young elf closed the door behind them and Adrien rushed to the window. He tried to open it and found it securely locked. The footsteps were closing in. He didn't have time for the delicate lock-picking spell. He stepped back and kicked the glass. Wasting no time, he cleared the shards away and gestured for Rafe to come to him.

"Go. Stay low and find somewhere safe to hide. I'll come for you soon." He pushed the boy out of the window. "Hide."

Rafe glared at him. He wanted to stand and fight. Just because he was small didn't mean he wasn't capable.

"Please, Rafe." Adrien looked at the door that the captors now pounded on. "Go."

The youngster decided that he wouldn't hide, but he would go into the forest. The boy was hatching a plan to sneak back into the house to free Adrien and rescue him. He saw his opportunity to prove himself to everyone and he wouldn't let that go.

The older elf formed his second short sword and braced himself for the fight. The door cracked before it collapsed under the next blow. A large man stormed into the room with his lips pulled into a grimace. He reached forward to grab Adrien's shoulder, but the elf plunged his sword into the man's stomach. There was no time to waste worrying about hurting people. These men had kidnapped him and potentially planned on killing him. Sometimes, blood had to be shed.

The man slumped with a gurgle. The remaining two men and a woman circled around Adrien as he stared them down while assessing their balance and movement.

"Stand down." A young woman with deep-green hair stepped into the room. "Now."

The people who had circled cast their eyes down and left the room. Adrien saw them waiting in the hallway, ready to continue the fight. He looked at the woman who clasped her hands behind her back and greeted him with a polite smile.

"I'm sorry for your accommodations here." She walked closer to him. "I'm afraid they misunderstood my intentions. Do you know who I am?"

"No." He side-stepped and moved closer to the exit. "Am I supposed to?"

Her smile turned sad. "My name is Mary. I'm your cousin." She brushed the dust off the single chair in the room and sat. "I'm sorry that your family has hidden so much from you. You see, they have lost their way. Guardians aren't what they used to be." She sighed. "We are the true guardians. We watch over those with Raven's blood as your family is supposed to do. Unfortunately, your family lost their way, and...well, they kill the wrong people."

Adrien raised an eyebrow and saw that the others had blocked the doorway entirely.

"We're the chosen few, and we wish you to join our ranks. You're a very talented guardian, Adrien. Your blood is pure, and we have felt the strength of your magic. It's such a shame to see your potential wasted on these awful people." She brushed some dust from her pants. "You will join us, won't you?"

He laughed a harsh, mocking laugh. "No." He spun his sword and prepared to reignite the fight and get out of there. "You're insane."

She pursed her lips. "We are the chosen and are giving you the opportunity of a lifetime." She stood. "You dare mock me?"

"No one has Raven's blood. That is some bizarre myth that has been spread through the groups like yours by egotistical and money-driven people. Let me guess, your leader is Gerard?"

The woman narrowed her eyes at him. "Yes."

Adrien smiled and felt victorious. His mother had told him about Gerard's group.

"Gerard is nothing more than a businessman. He has no desire to be a guardian or to protect people. Those with Raven's blood are merely people who have paid your boss an amount he deemed suitable." He looked at those standing in the doorway. "You bring shame on the title of guardian."

With that, he rushed the people blocking his path. He ducked low and swung his sword at the side of the woman's knee. She yelped in shock and pain. Adrien rolled away and sliced at the man's side. He clutched the wound and whispered a healing spell. The young elf was caught off guard by the other woman who threw a concussive blast of air at him. He collided with the far wall. The air was driven from his lungs and everything ached. His captors closed in around him.

Adrien refused to give in that easily. He stood and began his attack anew. The woman hadn't healed her knee and was slower than the others. He took advantage of that and blocked a blow from the sword of the broadest man before he bolted forward and slit the woman's throat. Her body had barely hit the floor when he leapt over it and ran into the hallway.

The elf had no idea where he was going. Footsteps thundered behind him and he called upon every shred of energy he had as he raced down the hallways and ran through the airy room that had alerted them of his impending escape. Something caught his eye out the window. It was enough to distract him, and his foot caught on a raised section of the well-worn red carpet. He tripped but caught himself.

That was enough for the woman to run into the room and cast a binding spell on him. Thick black ropes bound him from collarbone to ankle. He fell on his side as he tried to call his magic and free himself. Adrien struggled to calm his mind while his captors closed in around him. The broad man hauled him onto his shoulder and carried him into a small room with pea-green wallpaper, complete with delicate bright pink flowers. The man dropped him unceremoniously on the bare mattress in the corner.

"You will see our way of thinking." He turned away from the elf. "And you will join our ranks."

---

Adrien estimated he was there for thirty minutes or so before the man returned. Once again, he was hauled onto his shoulder and carried unceremoniously through the dilapidated house. His captor paused in front of a thick door with a raven carved into it. The woman from before opened the door and gestured toward the bed on the right side of the room.

She sat in a brocade chair with her legs crossed at the ankles. A delicate porcelain cup and saucer sat on a dark wood table. She picked them up and sipped at their contents.

When Adrien was alone with her, she began talking and he resumed his attempts to free himself. His magic simply wouldn't respond and exhaustion filled his bones and made every little movement difficult. The woman spoke in a clear, strong voice with the confidence that came from knowing he couldn't do a thing.

"I was like you once. When I was your age, I think. I thought that I knew the world and how it all worked. Then my eyes were opened, and I was initiated into the Ravens." She sighed with a blissful expression on her face. "Oh, how I fought at first. I had been tied up for a week while I thought my situation through. He was so patient with me. Each day, he returned and calmly explained the error of my ways. I finally began to see how right he was. The day of my initiation was one of the happiest of my life. They're my family. Our bonds are stronger than any blood family. We are bound by the need to protect those who cannot protect themselves."

"You are fools who run around and kill people because your money-hungry boss tells you to," Adrien spat.

The woman shook her head sadly. "I'm afraid you're the fool, dear Adrien. You see, the world is a dark and dangerous place. There will be a time in the not too distant future where things will change. There are small signs of it already, which is why we must protect the chosen. They are the key to our continued success and progress." She placed her cup and saucer down. "The Raven-born, those with the sacred Raven blood, will guide us through the darkness. We protect them from the cruel and harsh world around us. They blossom now and come into their evolved state. It is up to us to watch over them while they are more delicate. Yes, I have blood on my hands, but it is nothing compared to what will flow if we fail in our mission. The world will burn. We are the saviors. Everyone will see the good that we have done. You should be honored that you have been chosen to join us on this mission."

Adrien had been warned that their group was delusional, but he saw that they were also boring and fond of their own voices.

"The world will not burn. I don't know what you're talking about. You've been taken in by a con-man."

"Gerard is not a con-man. He is a god among men. How dare you speak to such—" She closed her eyes and calmed herself. "I was like you at first. It is my duty to show you the way. You have so much potential, Adrien. The potential to do such good in the world. Your family is cruel to have hidden you from your true path and kept you from the truth of everything. Allow me to open your eyes."

He sighed and closed his eyes. If he had to be stuck listening to her talk, he decided he might as well save his energy and hope his magic returned to him when the time was right.

# CHAPTER FORTY-FOUR

They were ready to break from the cover of the forest and rush toward the front door when a small boy with pale-blue eyes and light-blonde hair barreled toward them with a dagger clutched in his hand. He stopped in front of Raine.

"Are you here to save Adrien?" He gulped air. "I'm going to rescue him."

Raine looked at Librarian Decker, unsure whether this was another trick or spell.

"Have you seen Adrien?" the gnome asked as he walked toward the boy. "Inside the house?"

"Yes. He pushed me out of a window and said he'd come and rescue me later." The boy looked at the house. "I can't leave him there, though. I'm a guardian too."

The young elf set his shoulders back and brandished his dagger as though it were a long sword. "Will you help me, or do I have to get him out on my own?"

Raine smiled at his determination. She was sure he'd make his family proud.

"Do you know of a way to get into the house?" The head librarian nodded at the front door. "Somewhere better than that door?"

The boy frowned. "No. All the windows I saw were big and there were people in the room." He started toward the front door. "Go big or go home, my sister says."

Raine gathered her magic and ran through offensive spells in her mind. They had all strengthened their shields and were ready to dive into the fray. The head librarian led the way. He charged across the scruffy gravel driveway and launched a volley of fireballs at the door. Joe and William joined the assault. By the time they reached the entrance, there was nothing but a smoldering pile of ash where the door and frame had once been.

The gnomes dealt with the first group of people who attacked. They used an explosive wave of air that knocked the people down like bowling pins. Cameron launched himself at a smaller man who tried to hide around the corner and throw knives at them. The shifter sank his teeth into the man's wrist and shook it until it shattered. He ignored the punishing blows his adversary delivered to his ribs and turned to sink his teeth into the man's shoulder. He had wanted to bite his throat, but he couldn't reach it.

The man crumpled into a sobbing heap as blood dribbled between his fingers where he gripped his shoulder. Cameron rejoined Raine, satisfied that the man would no longer be a threat. Sara and Evie threw explosive balls of light at the incoming attackers to blind them. William,

Philip, and Raine all used the binding spells Professor Powell had taught them and bound them in heavy ropes.

The gnomes weren't as concerned about injuring the attackers. They sent curses to strike the tall, willowy elves in the chest. Librarian Decker didn't pause to watch as one slowly disintegrated into a line of glitter. He had neither the time nor the desire to try to keep the people alive. They had kidnapped one of his students and that made them enemy number one.

Once the first group of guards had been dispatched, they raced through the mansion and followed the white orb. They ran through a large ballroom with a faded red carpet stained with blood and mildew. The once grand room was covered in dust and grime. The orb led them up a narrow staircase near the back of the house where they bumped into the next group of defenders.

These were more prepared and almost succeeded in driving the students and gnomes back down the stairs with sharp-edged curses that filled their minds with darkness and pain. Joe helped the students cut through the curses while Librarian Decker pushed forward and maintained a rapid volley of his own curses against them. Once the students were back in fighting form, they called their magic and threw concussive spells at the attackers.

Raine was pleased to find that her magic flowed well and she remembered all the spells she had learned since she'd joined the school. Her concussive explosion hit an older woman directly in the face and sent her sprawling. She hit the wall behind her with a heavy thud. The group grew tired from the running and magic use, but they wouldn't leave there without Adrien.

Joe passed his chocolates around quickly. They ate while they ran after the orb through worn rooms full of dust and floral prints. The globe crashed against a heavy wooden door with the engraving of a raven on it. Having finished its task, it disappeared. The students threw blasts of fire and air at the door but these slipped off like water off a duck's back. Sara rolled her shoulders and stepped forward.

"I know how to break this. It's one Mom taught me." She raised her hands. "This is an old Japanese warding spell."

She gritted her teeth and formed a sharp blade in her mind. Focused now, she pushed her magic through the shape and looked for the kanji she knew would be present. This wasn't full kitsune magic and was simply a little something stolen from them. That meant the ward wasn't as strong as the one her sister had put around Sara's favorite art supplies last summer.

Sara found the kanji and drove her magic into them until they exploded. Once that was done, she sliced her magical blade through the layers and wards until there were none. Raine watched her friend with a great swell of pride as she saw the light around the door begin to dull. The ward finally broke entirely with a soft, crackling sound. Sara stepped back and the others threw every scrap of air and fire they had at the door.

It exploded forward and the someone inside shouted in surprise. A tall woman with red streaks in her pitch-black hair stood slowly. She pressed her red lips together into a thin line and brushed some dust off her emerald-green dress.

"That was rather rude." She raised an eyebrow. "You could have knocked."

"You kidnapped our friend." Raine looked at Adrien who writhed on the bed. "We're here to take him home."

"Oh, but he is home." The woman spoke in an acidic tone. "He will be a Raven protector."

Raine snorted. "This is how this will work. We'll unbind and take Adrien. You'll let us walk out of here. If you don't, you won't be walking anywhere, and we'll tell his family exactly where you're located." She smiled sweetly. "Which will it be?"

The woman threw a cluster of small knives at Raine's head. She ducked and rolled, popped back up, and threw a trio of fireballs at her adversary. Evie gritted her teeth and listened to the words of her grandmother. Sometimes, they really needed to stop thinking like healers and really kick some ass. Evie had always been careful and was a gentle soul at heart, but Adrien was in danger. The time for knocking the attackers out had passed. Now, it was time to really show them what they were capable of.

She dug deep into her magic and reached for the nature magic in the surrounding area. The state of disrepair of the house made it much easier to sink her mental fingertips into it. She called upon the plants and trees and watched with great pride as a mass of vines grew at an insane speed from the floor and around the woman. The vines encircled her legs and wound toward her chest. The woman hacked at them and tried to burn them, but the creepers were too swift. Evie pushed more of her magic into them and they grew inch-long curved thorns that sank into the woman's flesh as she struggled and raged against them.

The vines bound her chest and slowly squeezed the life out of her. Evie gave a satisfied nod and said, "Don't screw with healers," to herself.

Cameron had jumped onto the bed and now chewed on the bindings around Adrien. The elf attempted to use his magic to free himself from the inside, but he was so tired. Joe rushed over and shoved a chocolate bar in the elf's mouth. Adrien chewed and felt his magic return as he watched the gnome tackle a large opponent to the ground and curse him into a frozen state. The man gazed at the ceiling with his mouth hanging open and an eternal look of surprise fixed on his face.

Between Cameron and Adrien, they managed to loosen the bindings. Once free, the elf called his sword and helped Philip cut down a particularly skilled older elf. The wizard danced to the side and kept the man occupied with blinding shots of light and smaller fireballs. Adrien sliced into the man's muscle and bone and cut him down with a fury that he had never felt before.

The woman had talked and talked while he had been bound. She had sat in her brocade chair and talked with such pride about the innocent people they had slaughtered. The small children they had stolen from their parents and the humans they had cut down without a care in the world. They called themselves guardians and claimed to protect those who were worthy, but Adrien knew they were filthy excuses for people. They were a blight on the world.

The group was careful to only do as much damage as was strictly necessary. Only two people had been killed when they gathered around their friend and hugged him until he begged to be able to breathe again.

"Thank you. All of you." Adrien smiled at the group. "You will make your family very proud, Rafe."

The younger boy hadn't been able to weave magic or cut people down the way the older students had, but Adrien had seen the way he had controlled the movements of their enemies. Rafe had played an instrumental part in the fight, even if the others hadn't seen him.

They moved through the house with their wands up in case they had missed someone. When they stepped out into the forest, they breathed a sigh of relief and began the walk back toward the gnomes' cars. They'd saved Adrien and everything was back as it was supposed to be.

## CHAPTER FORTY-FIVE

Raine held her head high as Professor Powell, Agent Connor, and the headmistress looked at her and her friends. The gnomes were present too, and Librarian Decker's poppy continuously blew raspberries. Ms. Berens sighed.

"You snuck into the kemana, which resulted in Adrien being kidnapped. You then felt that you were in the best position to get him back." She looked at the group. "There is no reason why I shouldn't give you a year's detention."

Raine had been prepared for this.

"With respect, headmistress, we acted in the way that was best for Adrien. Yes, I admit that we were wrong to sneak into the kemana. That said, we acted responsibly and used everything that Professor Powell has taught us over the last year. My understanding is that this school was created by the government to train magically gifted students to step into roles that allow us to protect and aid those without magic."

She didn't look away from the headmistress. "We put our training to use and demonstrated that you and the professors have taught us appropriately. Had we tried to find you and explained the situation, Adrien may have been seriously injured or worse. Librarian Decker and his second in command, Joe, provided us with guidance and aid which ensured that we were as safe as possible throughout the entire process."

Agent Connor tried to hold back his smile. He had known that Raine was the right choice for the agency, and she had demonstrated that clearly here.

The head librarian rocked on his feet. "I understand that we overstepped some boundaries. But there will always be enemies of the school and those who attend it. It's not unreasonable to expect the students to use what you teach them here. But Raine is right. They put everything they have been trained to do to good use to save a fellow student. What more can you ask from them?"

Mara tried to quash the pride she felt for the students and everything that they had accomplished. Adrien's parents weren't entirely happy with how everything had come together. They had been glad he had been returned in one piece, but the fact that he was taken in the first place understandably upset them. She had spent an hour talking to them about every precaution they had taken. Adrien was a skilled combatant in his own right, but he was still his parents' youngest.

"You will participate in extra classes with Professor Powell." Agent Connor looked sternly at Raine. "We do not agree with your methods, but the outcome is favorable. We understand that your aim is to become an FBI agent, but remember that agents keep their superiors in the loop."

Raine tried to restrain a victorious expression. "Understood." She nodded. "Thank you."

"You will spend the next two days helping the pixies scrub the kitchen from top to bottom." Professor Powell looked at them. "Expect to use toothbrushes. That kitchen will shine like it has never shone before. And there will be no magic aids."

With that, the students were sent away. Mara looked at the gnomes with a small smile.

"Thank you for watching over them, Leo." She sighed softly. "I think Adrien's parents would have removed him and his brother from the school had you not been there."

The gnome shrugged. "It was a good adventure. I love the library, but it was nice to be out in the world again." He grinned. "We made the world a little brighter. The Raven blood clan have been shut down, and three other children they kidnapped have been found and returned to their families. The last I heard, the surviving members of the clan have been arrested on outstanding murder warrants. The methods were less than ideal, but you have to admit that the results were really very good."

Mara sighed again and Xander put his arm around her shoulders. "Please don't encourage Raine and her friends to have more adventures."

The head librarian laughed. "I will do my best, but I can't make any promises."

Raine knelt in front of the main oven as she scrubbed the closest corner. It had taken almost two hours, but the interior began to shine. She had needed three separate cleaning products and was on her second scrubbing brush, but the progress was visible now. Her arms and shoulders ached and she was sure she'd gained muscle from all the scrubbing and cleaning.

She only had to spend another ten minutes on the final section and she'd be finished. The pixies had put on a radio station that mixed rock with pop and it made the day go by so much faster. Tori and the other pixies insisted that the students stop and have regular dance breaks. Overall, as cleaning went, Raine almost enjoyed it. Of course, she would have preferred they use magic, but there was something satisfying about scrubbing. She put her back into it and watched as everything came up truly spotless.

"Don't tell my mom I did this. She'll expect me to clean her kitchen." Philip grinned. "One kitchen is enough for me."

"My mom won't let me in the kitchen so I'm safe." Sara laughed. "I suspect she'll ban me entirely if I tell her about those sentient cupcakes."

"I still can't believe that happened." Evie laughed. "I've been terrified to make cupcakes since."

"They tasted really good." Raine grinned. "I think I'll skip the magic bit when I make them for Uncle Jerry, though."

"My younger cousins would love them." Evie stood and stretched her back. "Although I don't want to know what would happen when they did get stale."

"That sounds like something from a horror movie." William rinsed his cloth. "Is there a movie like that? If so, we need to add it to our list."

"I'll do some digging." Philip stood up, triumphant. His section was immaculate. "I'm done."

They had reached the end of their second day of scrubbing the kitchen and it was immaculate. Every tile gleamed, and the floor was clean enough to eat off. As far as punishments went, Raine felt that was one of the better ones.

"I'm done." Sara stood and did a little dance. "The oven shines."

Raine finished scrubbing the last little spot and joined her friend in her dance around the central table. Cameron had finished his designated area ten minutes before and had a detailed discussion about cookie types with Tori.

"Wait, you can really add lavender to cookies too?" Cameron frowned. "I had no idea you could put it in so many things."

"Oh, yes. The variety of cookies and cupcakes available is almost unlimited." Tori pulled out her huge cookbook. It was a good six inches thick and bulged with recipes. "See. Here are your nut-based options. Personally, I'm not a fan of coffee and walnut cookies. I think that's better suited to a cake. Some people enjoy them, though. White chocolate and macadamia are a classic."

"Did someone say white chocolate and macadamia nuts?" Sara bounced over. "They are the queen of cookies."

"Raisin oatmeal. Hands down." William stretched his back. "Nothing can beat them."

Everyone turned to look at him agape.

"No way!"

"Blasphemy!"

"Do you have taste buds?"

William laughed. "Choc chip is boring." He folded his arms. "No one can say they're the best."

"Cranberry and white chocolate is to die for." Evie put her arm through William's. "But I forgive you for your oatmeal and raisin cookies."

Once Adrien finished, the pixies turned the music up and formed some sparkling grapefruit juice for everyone to drink.

"To a long and fulfilling summer." Tori lifted her glass. "And all the most wonderful food."

Everyone cheered and toasted to that. Raine enjoyed her grape juice and felt a deep happiness fill her bones.

---

Sara sat on her suitcase while Evie tried to pull the zip around.

"How much extra stuff did you pack in here? I'm not sure this will work."

"Only a few paints and paint brushes. Oh, and some pastels." Sara grinned. "Maybe some charcoal."

Evie laughed. "Can you squeeze more into it? Or will it burst?"

Sara chewed on her bottom lip. "I'm pretty sure that the moment I touch that zip, the entire bag will explode."

Everyone laughed.

"Well, can you leave any of it here?" Raine looked at the bulging suitcase. "The charcoal maybe?"

Sara sighed melodramatically. "I guess I can leave some of the paint. I can always get more back home." She hopped off the suitcase which strained against the zip. "The charcoal is for my sister, so I'll definitely take that with me."

Evie backed away as Sara opened the suitcase. To everyone's surprise, it didn't explode. A few tubes of paint tumbled out, but it wasn't a disaster.

Raine had packed her bags the day before and she didn't have anything special to take back with her. She had managed to add a couple of books into her backpack but there was still plenty of room should she need it. Evie had filled hers with baking implements which the pixies had given her.

Sara put the extra paint onto her bed and they began the process of zipping the suitcase again. It was a joint effort, but they managed it more easily that time. Sara used an air spell to help her lift the case onto the ground. She was very glad it was a wheeled case, although she still didn't look forward to getting it down all the stairs at the train station.

Cameron slung his backpack over his shoulder and helped William carry his case down the stairs. He looked forward to spending the entire summer with the half-Ifrit at his pack home. He had planned fun activities for his friend, including camping and white-water rafting. William couldn't keep the grin off his face at the thought. The shifter had been a fantastic friend and made him feel welcome and helped him increase his confidence. He was so happy to have met him.

Adrien knew his summer would be full of training and preparation, and he relished that. Having been kidnapped had bruised his ego but he would not let it happen again. He had worked on the unbinding spells every evening and couldn't wait for the extra lessons with Professor Powell.

Philip had plans to do charity work through the summer. He'd done a lot of research and found two charities in his local area that worked hard to help less advantaged kids get a good start in life. He had also found a tutor who would help him with history, so he could improve his grade for the next year.

The guys walked down the main stairs and met the girls at the bottom. They were almost the last ones to leave. William could see Mrs. Beasley and her jitney in the driveway, waiting for them. Evie strode up to William with a broad smile on her face. His eyes went wide as he wasn't sure where this was going. He really liked Evie, but he didn't quite know how to act around her. While he liked being close to her, he still felt awkward and completely unsure of himself.

Evie knew that he didn't have the confidence to make the next move. Luckily, she'd been raised by a group of strong women, so she unhesitatingly wrapped her arms around William's neck. She grinned at him as she leaned in slowly and kissed him softly.

"I'm officially making you my boyfriend," she whispered in his ear.

William blushed furiously and grinned as happiness filled him. The summer really couldn't get any better now.

Sara clapped and grinned. "You guys make such an adorable couple." She ran to them and hugged them tightly. "I'm so happy for you."

Cameron put his arm around Raine's waist and quietly kissed her cheek. He would miss her over the summer, but he hoped they'd be able to see each other at least once. Agent Connor cleared his throat and the group turned.

"Mrs. Beasley has asked me to tell you that if you don't get your butts on that jitney in the next two minutes, you'll be walking. She would like to begin her summer vacation."

Sara hugged Cameron and Raine tightly before she rolled her overstuffed suitcase out to the jitney. Agent Connor took pity on her and followed her so he could lift it into the luggage hold for her. Cameron cupped Raine's cheek in his hand and kissed her softly. He looked into her eyes and smiled as he drank in every detail of her.

"We'll talk every day." Raine leaned into him and rested her head on his shoulder. "I'll see you in no time at all."

He kissed her temple and walked away. He hated doing it, but he was pretty sure Mrs. Beasley wasn't joking. The walk to the train station wasn't a short one.

The friends all wished each other a great summer and promised to stay in touch. Agent Connor approached Raine when they had left.

"Ready?"

"Yeah."

"It's been a hell of a year hasn't it?"

Raine smiled. "It has. I can't wait to see what the next one holds."

Little did Raine know that her adventures had only just begun.

The End

An Artifact stolen from a secret vault. Hounds of hell unleashed on the students. Dorvu to the rescue! Raine's adventure continues in <u>Special Witch of the FBI.</u>

FREE BOOKS!

 WARNING:
**The Troll is now in charge.**
And he's giving away free books
if you sign-up!

Join the only newsletter hosted by a Troll! Get sneak peeks, exclusive giveaways, behind the scenes content, and more. PLUS you'll be notified of special **one day only fan pricing** on new releases.

CLICK HERE

or visit: https://marthacarr.com/read-free-stories/

**For Hire: Teachers for special school in Virginia countryside.**

Must be able to handle teenagers with special abilities.

Cannot be afraid to discipline werewolves, wizards, elves and other assorted hormonal teens.

Apply at the School of Necessary Magic.

**Meet the first Freshmen class!**

# AVAILABLE ON AMAZON RETAILERS

It's been raining in Austin, Texas like the map shifted and we're really Portland, instead. The overcast skies remind me of my days in Chicago – not the wide-open blue skies that are typical of big ol' Texas. It's good for putting my head down and writing, which is also good because there's a lot of books coming out in the beginning of the year. Time to get to gettin'.

Good thing I like writing and making up magical beings (who might swear, we'll see). The end of the year approaches, and soon it'll be time for black eyed peas and a piece of silver by your plate. First one for good luck and the second for good fortune. Growing up, Dad would give each of us a dime.

This past year has been a big year full of extremes. A lot of new books, a little cancer, and a new house, mixed in with the Offspring's engagement to Jackie. Each of those has a longer story behind them and they all overlapped each other. Like I said, it's been a big year...

But the biggest event was that my oldest sister, Diana died unexpectedly after a short illness. It's a strange thing to lose a sibling. Standing by her bed, I kept thinking of our younger versions (kept picturing her red hair and very determined stare) and how much we had planned for the world. I didn't see it ending just yet.

She was ten years older than I am and my hero from an early age.

Diana knew she wanted to be a doctor from the get-go and went about it quietly and with a certainty that made it seem like it had to happen. Mix in her love of DC comics – there were packing crates full of comics when I was little – and Star Trek and you can see why I admired her so much. It helped me see the world as a giant place full of wondrous things from an early age. It would serve me well later when life got tough to remember that in the end, life is beautiful.

In her honor, I am going to keep on trudging with that same attitude and keep an eye out for the wonder, sharing it as much as possible with others, like all of you.

So, on to the next year – 2019 here we come! Here's what I know so far –

• I'll be sponsoring an online gaming tournament. Any gamers out there? Details coming
• More events at the Veterans Center
• Good ol' fashioned book tour to meet more fans across the country (hopefully some of you live in Buffalo, because Niagara Falls is on my bucket list, just sayin')
• Loads more books – including The Peabrain Adventures, and a non-fiction on success and getting out of our own way called Indie Writer

• Not moving...

• Just joined something called Camp Gladiators (little afraid of this one... doing it anyway) and will be working out more in 2019

• Heading out into the dating world – have a bet with Stephen Campbell who can conquer their mountain first. Mine is dating – at least 4 with the same person and his is finishing his next thriller. Photographer is headed over this weekend so Campbell better be writing!

• Spend more time with family and friends and get to know Austin even better – open up this new house for more dinners and parties and gatherings of all kind

That's it – and it's more than enough. Probably, by the end of 2019 a lot will have happened (Anderle will have a wild idea and of course I'll say yes, and off we'll go...), and it will be another big year. Looking forward to all of it. More adventures to follow.

THANK YOU for not only reading this story but these *Author Notes* as well.

(I think I've been good with always opening with "thank you." If not, I need to edit the other *Author Notes*!)

RANDOM (*sometimes*) THOUGHTS?

So honoring Martha's kind of year-in-review post, I'll mention a few things I have going on, and some of my thoughts in general.

• From 2016 go 2018, Martha went from a traditionally published author to a full time Indie focused powerhouse, collaborating on umpteen kajillion series and did all of that while still holding down a full time job. From that success, she moved homes and bought the house of her dreams. I'm very happy to have played a part in that effort, but I point back to her and 'I heard Universe, he swears he said series' comment.

• I'm selling my house in Texas, and I'm damned envious that she is all done with selling hers.

• I have three guys and I hope like hell none of them get married, financed or anything in 2019. Two are 19 and the 26 year old (I think) isn't going to surprise me. I suspect he might be someone who is happy marrying in his 30's.

• I"m not ready to be a grandfather. Period. So, I don't want any surprises please oh please in 2019!

• I successfully (so far) created multiple new series by myself, or in collaboration in 2018 (Brownstone, School(s), Animus, and now the ZOO series. I have more series on tap, and hope to get a handle on how to write these author note updates, as I'm going to have a bunch to do!

• Bali in January (20Books), London (?) in March, SFWA (Nebulas) in Spring, Edinburgh (20Books) in Summer followed by Worldcon 2019. Beijing book fair sometime in there then Frankfurt book fair followed by 20Booksto50k Vegas in November. Lot's of travel, and looking to see what we can cut out in 2020.

• Writing….Lot's and Lot's of writing.

• Collaborating…Lot's and Lot's of Collaborating with existing authors and new ones coming into fruition in 2019.

• Learning how to take a few Sunday's off.

• I want to read more.

• I want to use VR instead of a large monitor.

• I want to learn the basics of Blender 2.8.

HOW TO MARKET FOR BOOKS YOU LOVE

We are able to support our efforts with you reading our books, and we appreciate you doing this!

If you enjoyed this or ANY book by any author, especially Indie-published, we always appreciate if you make the time to review a book, since it lets other readers who might be on the fence to take a chance on it as well.

AROUND THE WORLD IN 80 DAYS

One of the interesting (at least to me) aspects of my life is the ability to work from anywhere and at any time. In the future, I hope to re-read my own *Author Notes* and remember my life as a diary entry.

Texas.

Right now, I'm fighting off sleep because we took the redeye from Las Vegas to Texas to talk with some contractors to fix stuff around our Texas home. (I mentioned above we are selling it.)

I hate …. HATE … having to sell a home. If it wasn't such a huge risk to have it without using it much, I'd be too tempted to keep it.

For no good reason.

I once thought I would enjoy living on a boat because it forced you to reduce your junk and learn how to use really small tools (among other small things.). I know live in a condo with about 2-3x the amount of space in a small boat and I've learned a very valuable lesson.

I'm way too lazy to learn how to live on a boat. There goes my ability to delude myself and romanticize living on a boat. I now want a nice sized house again (not the size of this one in Texas, it is too big. BUT, something where I can have all the man-cave I want. And then another 100 extra square feet.)

Oh, and closets. My wife has stolen all of them practically. The master bedroom in the Condo has 2 closets, 2 sinks and I don't get a square inch of any of it. I have exactly 1 nightstand and half the bed.

And I'd better be happy with that.

FAN PRICING

If you would like to find out what LMBPN is doing and the books we will be publishing, just sign up at http://lmbpn.com/email/. When you sign up, we notify you of books coming out for the week, any new posts of interest in the books and pop culture arena, and the fan pricing on Saturday.

Ad Aeternitatem,
Michael Anderle

OTHER SERIES IN THE ORICERAN
UNIVERSE:


SCHOOL OF NECESSARY MAGIC
THE DANIEL CODEX SERIES
I FEAR NO EVIL
THE UNBELIEVABLE MR. BROWNSTONE
THE LEIRA CHRONICLES
REWRITING JUSTICE
THE KACY CHRONICLES
MIDWEST MAGIC CHRONICLES
SOUL STONE MAGE
THE FAIRHAVEN CHRONICLES

OTHER BOOKS BY JUDITH BERENS

OTHER BOOKS BY MARTHA CARR

# CONNECT WITH THE AUTHORS

## Martha Carr Social

Website: http://www.marthacarr.com

Facebook:
https://www.facebook.com/groups/MarthaCarrFans/

## Michael Anderle Social

Michael Anderle Social
Website:
http://www.lmbpn.com

Email List:
http://lmbpn.com/email/

Facebook Here:
https://www.facebook.com/TheKurtherianGambitBooks/